W. H. (William Henry) Bogart

Who goes there?

or, Men and events

W. H. (William Henry) Bogart

Who goes there?
or, Men and events

ISBN/EAN: 9783337414108

Printed in Europe, USA, Canada, Australia, Japan

Cover: Foto ©Andreas Hilbeck / pixelio.de

More available books at **www.hansebooks.com**

WHO GOES THERE?

OR,

MEN AND EVENTS.

BY

"SENTINEL."

"Now is the stately column broke,
The beacon light is quenched in smoke;
The trumpet's silver voice is still;
The warder silent on the hill."
— Scott.

NEW YORK:
Carleton, Publisher, 413 Broadway.
M DCCC LX VI.

THIS VOLUME

Is Dedicated to

FREDERICK G. FOSTER,

Of the City of New York,

IN

UNFADING MEMORIES OF KINDNESS.

PREFACE.

This volume is the record of personal recollections, or of reminiscence, related to me by those who had themselves known or seen or had enjoyed extraordinary opportunity of information of the persons delineated. As far as possible, that only has been related which is not elsewhere told.

In its preparation, I have been most conscious into what a great division of intellectual labor it was just entering, and how many gentlemen there are whose range of sight and hearing of the world's worthies had been so extensive, as that they positively owed their fellow-men the duty of perpetuating their delightful and copious recollections.

I have avoided the time immediately past, because the vision of character is gentlest through the mist of time; and, except in -a very few brief words, have confined the action of the volume alone to those whose record death had sealed. There are illustrious men living in our midst to whom abler narrators will bring the offering of history.

WILLIAM H. BOGART.

CONTENTS.

WHO GOES THERE?

CHAPTER I.

WASHINGTON — LAFAYETTE.

HERE is, of course, in these pages no design of writing any personal memoirs. My life has been but one of the millions, without place, or influence, or power, who form part of the world's great census. It is in the position of an observer of other men, and of the events of my times, that this narrative is penned; and if, in the necessity of the relation, I am compelled to allude to what I have myself seen or known, it is only as of the use of words which could not be avoided. I have chosen the title of this book as corresponding with the signature which, for a long series of years of journalism, I used. SENTINEL was accidentally my *nom de plume*, and, as once adopted, it was always retained, and there are many memories of very kind friends associated with it. What is to

be written will not always be of individuals known
to me. In many instances I have studied to
know by the living witnesses what was by them
known of great men in whose cycle they had
lived, and of whose language or actions they
could relate that which was interesting; and of
the very great of this earth, who as certainly are the
very few, nearly all detail *is* interesting. That was
a truth long since enunciated by Voltaire, and as
keenly restated by our own, almost greatest, phi-
losopher-statesman, John Quincy Adams. It is
not a word of sentimentalism or affectation when
the French savans desired to know what were the
trivial daily habits of the Isaac Newton whose
grandeur of thought they appreciated. We may,
by the minute touches of the picture, declare the
hand of the master. Excepting Lafayette, all the
great names of the Revolution were in the roll of
death before I felt interest in history; or, if others
lived, they were in the seclusion of their own
distant homes. Yet those who remembered them
in their old age, were, although mature men or
women themselves, active in our circle; and it
was to me a pursuit, of which I thought I saw the
true and great value, to hear their delineation of
the look, or word, or way of the illustrious,
especially as they always observed them as illustrious men, and in more or less consciousness that

what they saw or heard from them was of value.

I have assumed incredulity as the best preparation for truth in all these conferences with tradition, because I knew that as men were in reality of high distinction, and as the time between the incident narrated of them and that at which we hear it is long, so does the imagination add, or the memory lose, of precision. The past had no press, to see even the most minute occurrence and make record of the progress of whatever fixes for the hour the public gaze. Hence it is, that all before the era of the modern development of journalism was left to the precarious accuracy or industry of unorganized labor, and the history of kings is about as likely to be truthful when Scott's romance relates it, as it is in colored annals of those who wrote to make a hero, not to record what the monarch had really said or done. In our day, Macaulay and Motley have insisted upon truth first, and hence, touched by their serious hand of verity, certain names of men have gone into the first rank of ability and worth in public service. I recollect hearing Fennimore Cooper lament over the utter unreliability of evidence, as applied even to occurrences where exactness might seem to have been easy; and said he, " Now, would not you suppose that when a newspaper stated that a ship had sailed on a particular day, that might be considered as true; yet, here in relation to this ship, she did not sail till a month after the date mentioned."

All of us have a little imagination, and perhaps most of those who know the value of observation have it in large degree; so we like, when we are telling of our glimpses at the dramatic pages of the world and the world's masters, to give our narrative the glitter and grace of gilding and drapery. I have believed thus of others, and possibly it may be just that which my readers may say is foible or defect in my own narratives.

There is a degree of safety in speaking of the dead. I find that Dr. Sprague said to me, when commencing his great book, the Annals of the American Pulpit, that he could biographize no living man. He waited to see *how careers are closed.* We are taught what to say of them, and especially what *not* to say, by the familiar adage whose Latin words have prevented many a pen from writing obituaries in very black ink. Our flattery of those whose life we know not to deserve it, has made the necrology of this country a kind and pleasant fable, and we only do not deceive ourselves. We *know* that the saints and statesmen we have delineated do not so deserve canonization and statues, as our eulogies have claimed, and we

have something of contempt for the popular rule of
nothing but praise. And if it be dangerous in the
case of the dead, to invade thus, how much more
so in that of the living! What is said against men in
political warfare is not considered as a record of ac-
cusation; it is only the arrow barbed or poisoned
for the purpose of the hour, and we think it almost
bad taste that Mr. Jefferson bound in a volume,
for his library, the hard things said of him — its
title-page the one expressive word, Libels; for we
know that his fame is at this hour a national property and a national glory. Would even Mr. Jefferson have taken pleasantly a just analysis of
his character, shown to him as it really appeared
to impartial delineation? I doubt it. He would
have been far more offended at some error that
was noted, than gratified at the good recorded.
Or, if *he* would not have been disturbed, it would
only have been because he was Mr. Jefferson, a
very great man. This risk we must run if we
write of living men, and can but hope that some
after hour of life's retrospect may show them that
the picture was not intended for a public scandal or
a caricature. Even the autobiographies of men do
not expose the truth of character. Every man
keeps within himself an inner room, of which conscience only keeps the key; and either from
dread or good taste, that remains the secret cham-

ber whose history he commits to remorse or repentance, asking, most of all, the oblivion of forgiveness.

There is, in our country, one era, the history of which is just enough blended with a romantic thought to give it perpetual interest. It is that of the Revolution, as we all call it, though General Washington spoke of it as the affair with Great Britain. Old manners and old customs had not all faded out; the ways of the simpler-hearted people of the past were in it; its republicanism was in all the earnest of a new theory, where it was safe to predict almost ideal virtue, and yet it came with us respectfully and respectably, after a long lineage of loyalty. Our fathers fought stoutly against the Royal Family, whom, but a very few years before, they had as vigorously defended; and the new portraits of the handsome Virginian General, and of the orators and philosophers of Massachusetts, were in the same house, and only in a different room, with those of William Pitt, of the Georges and Charlottes and Sophias, of Wolfe, of Lady Fanny Murray, of all those that, to this hour, one can find in the relics preserved in many a house in Albany. Something of stateliness crowned the hour of independence, and we did not at once become square and sharp and practical. Recollecting that the active men of the Revolution were those whose birth-date was in the early or the middle of the last century, it is not at all strange that they made their old memories the tinge of coloring to all their new and more vivid acting; and they retained, in the period to which the memory of men living a few years since connected us, something of the dramatic, something clothed in the equipage of the times. when colonies considered themselves as children of the British empire, and not as its vassals. We need, sometimes, to think of this, to make real to ourselves the great fact of our history,— that our Revolution was not an easy choice of a new theory of government, but the greatest of sacrifices, the separation from all the home and heart associations of centuries.

Of course, of all the names of our history, and especially of the formation of that history, the centre, and none near him, is that of Washington. It is quite likely we do persist in looking at him in a glorious haze, and refuse to see shadows that existed. Carlyle recently told an American that *he*, even he, Mr. Thomas Carlyle, intended "to take down that land-surveyor." We can all smile at this, as we can at any attempt to make any fracture or even abrasion of our statue. There he is, as pure as he was powerful, and calumny dies before him. We have — all of us have, differ on

2

what else we may — a settled satisfaction about Washington. He is not the man concerning whom we lie awake in fear that some discovered letter, some unfolded archive, some sudden witness shall reverse the judgment of the age. There is no Simanca whose old manuscripts have reserved, in faithful keeping, unwelcome truths. Soldier and statesman and gentleman, we are willing to let the coldest critic mouse around Mount Vernon. *His* grandeur is of the things time and truth have agreed shall be permanent.

I have sought every opportunity to converse with men who knew General Washington. Of course it could only be of the very few living in my day that it could be said that they had personally known him, especially in anything like lengthened conversation. In the testimony of all, perhaps that which made deepest impression was the dignity of the man. This they all said of him, and this testimony could not have been thus universal but as a reflection of the truth.

And, beginning these personal and derived reminiscences with this illustrious name, let it be understood that I relate only what I have seen or heard, keeping clear, if I can, of what is already of record, though aware that, in some cases, what was stated to me may have been previously told to others. My chief regret is, that in more instances

I did not fully appreciate the value of the men I met,— the events I witnessed.

It is not strange that the personal appearance of Washington was that which was best remembered; for it is the first and strongest impression; indeed, it is about all that the mere observer had opportunity to know. I have said that there was a universal testimony to his grandeur of mien and carriage, — yet that must be modified; for one of the most distinguished of all whose conversation respecting Washington I heard,— Josiah Quincy,— said he did not think him as majestic as reported, but spoke in special admiration of Gouverneur Morris's elegance,— a remark coming from him which gives additional interest to that memorandum in Mr. Morris's diary, which asserts that he stood to Houdon for the body of that statue which is everywhere considered as the *vraisemblance* of Washington. Mr. Everett did not believe this, and Judge Marshall's declaration of the entire fidelity of the statue strengthens this disbelief; yet, as both Washington and Morris were elegant men, it may be near the verity. John Van Zandt, himself a quaint and precise representative of the old business-man, suited to old ways, to the easy and limited life of other years, had very distinct recollection of seeing the General, or, as he then was, the President, riding in great state, as it would now be called, —

his coach with six horses, himself dressed in drab, and the object of universal attention, — Mr. Van Zandt, remembering the very natural occurrence. that he left a store in Broadway, New York, where he was at the moment, to run down the street the better to see him.   He said the President did not bow to the people, but remained erect and stern. This is not quite in our idea of his courtesy, though his was not excessive manner, and it may well be that at the moment when Mr. Van Zandt saw him he was fatigued.   When the Prince of Wales came up the streets of Hamilton, C. W., while the crowd cheered all around him, he did not at the time acknowledge it.   I watched him closely, and thought it out of good manners, but, afterward, justly reflected that he must be greatly wearied even in the profusion of hospitality ; and the seeming discourtesy of Washington may have been thus occasioned. Mr. Van Zandt saw and talked accurately, and was not likely to be imaginative in his recollections.

Philip Church, of Alleghany, a high-bred gentleman of great culture, graced the annals of Western New York by his residence there.   In very early life, he was, through his kindred to General Schuyler, an officer under Alexander Hamilton in the *quasi* war with France, at the close of the last century, — a war which the Federalists called the Pro-

visonal war, and the Democrats " the Provision-eat-
ing war," but which we, removed from their partisan
disputes, can see was a brave testimony to all the
world, that young as was our nation it would dare
all for the right ; and, better than that, that we saw
the hideous, the Satanic character of the French
Revolution.   He spoke in glowing language about
Washington, declaring him the most dignified and
inspiring man he ever met, and related the strength
of Hamilton's admiration for him, — that to him,
Alexander Hamilton, one of the impressive and
sublime features of his character was that he governed himself by his impartial judgment of what
was right even against friendship and prejudice.
Hamilton urged upon Mr. Church to recollect above
all things in his intercourse with the General to be
punctual ; that virtue being, if possible, in excess
with him, and its infraction being a cause of temporary alienation even between Washington and
his very right hand, — Hamilton himself.

Dr. John Miller, of Truxton, dined at the table of
President Adams with him, taken there by Dr.
Rush, of whom he was a student.   He was dressed
then in gray, — an example for the encouragement
of domestic manufactures ; and the impression on
the memory of the doctor was equally correct of
the stately gentleman.

And, indeed, this characteristic derives additional

proof from the very exceptions. Mr. Verplanck
says of events, — not from personal knowledge, but
from sources which none knew better than himself
how to appreciate, — that when Washington visited
the Lakes, in company with James Fairlie and
General Knox, he seemed to them to lay aside his
gravity and to enter into the *abandon* of the moment, even leaning back in his seat and laughing,
to the surprise of Knox ; and it will be remembered
that Knox was his life-long intimate.

Old Dr. Morse, of Watertown, near Boston, told
me that he remembered that in the procession, at
the reception of General Washington at that city,
they were kept in the common for an hour, waiting
the settlement of a question of precedence between
lawyers and doctors ; but this must have been all
forgotten by the doctor in his sense of the General's conduct on the occasion, for he considered him
as the very mirror of courtesy.

It was long remembered that when Washington
was on his western journey, — probably on the
way from Albany to Schenectady, — his own riding was so urgent and rapid, that the horsemen
with him could not keep up with him.

Albert Gallatin was especially interesting in his
conversation respecting the Pater Patriæ. He
was a young, enthusiastic foreigner, coming to our
country with all the theoretical, book ideas of a

complete republicanism, and viewing men and circumstances somewhat sharply, as they were in con-
sistency with, or in variation from, that standard,
by which, until it saw with greater sense, Europe
insisted upon judging the young republic. Men
read in classical fiction, dignified and disguised by
the name of history, about what philosophers
dreamed should be a republic (and which it never
was), and gave to America all the benefit or criticism of their dreamings. Mr. Gallatin talked
delightfully, with a clearness of statement and
exactness of manner, as if he knew himself that
what he said was valuable. He met the General
at a hut in the forest, where a party of officers and
surveyors were, under the direction of Washington,
seeking to ascertain what was the most available
route for a desired road across the mountain.
Maps were produced and evidence given, the lines
traced, and the General heard and looked on in
silence. To Mr. Gallatin's young and quick mind,
the result of the evidence seemed conclusive, and
he rather abruptly or inconsiderately exclaimed,
" Why, General, there can be no difficulty about .
it.   That " — naming a particular line — " that
is the right way for the road." Mr. Gallatin said
that the officers around him looked at him in surprise and displeasure, as if the interruption were a
rude one. But the General only looked up at him,

and then, for about eight minutes (such was Mr. Gallatin's precision of relation), continued his silence, and then said, " Mr. Gallatin, you are right." It was something, at the risk of a little infraction of the stately order of things, to have heard these words from George Washington.

Either that interview or subsequent knowledge of him gave Mr. Gallatin the impression that the first President was cold in his affections beyond the usual reticence even of isolated men ; for he stated with earnestness that he believed General Washington loved but one person ; and that one was Lafayette.

Mr. Francis Granger said it was traditional in the federal capital that one man was found not awed by the presence of the great founder of that city. While the President was procuring the ground for the city which was to be the seat of government, he had but little difficulty in obtaining the necessary releases, except in one instance. Mr. James Byrnes was the owner of a lot or tract which it was advisable should be included in the plan. The general had various conferences with Mr. Byrnes, who was especially obstinate, and resisted all the reasoning and persuasions of the great man. Unused to opposition, Washington turned upon him and said, as only he could say it, " Mr. James Byrnes ! what would your land have been worth if I had not placed this city on the Potomac ? " Byrnes was not crushed; but, undismayed, coolly turned to him and said, " George Washington, what would *you* have been worth *if you had not married the widow Custis ?* "

Mr. Thomas Handasyde Perkins talked very pleasantly about the General. He had visited Mount Vernon as the companion, and, in some sense, guardian of George Washington Lafayette, with whom he had come from Paris, to bring him to the safety of America out of the Red Sea of revolutionary cruelty. Washington received him very kindly, and after the evening's conversation, at an early hour, proposed retirement, and, taking up a flat candlestick, conducted Mr. Perkins to his room. " I think," said Mr. Perkins, gayly, " I must be the only man now living, who was lighted to bed by General Washington."

It impressed me very strongly, that, in this conversation, Mr. Perkins said that he found the streets of Paris, during this bitterness of revolutionary cruelty, when the Place de Greve had its daily victims, more quiet, and, he thought, more safe, than even those of New York.

While going to Boston, to attend the celebration of the laying of the top-stone of Bunker Hill Monument, I found Harrison Gray Otis at that most delicious of all hotels, " Warriner's "— the old Warriner's. He had come thither, he said, to escape the crowd of the festival. He talked about seeing Washington at Philadelphia, while in attendance on the convention that framed the Federal Constitution, and he shared the general impression of the presence and carriage of this superb man; and Mr. Otis's testimony, supposing it to have been a correct one, is valuable; for Mr. Otis was a man who was not disposed preeminently to value other men. What a brilliant, showy, but over-mannered man Mr. Otis seemed, as I saw him on that evening! William Kent once said to me he was a very magician in his eloquence. He was in excellent humor this evening, as most men were around such luxury of entertainment as the unequalled Warriner gave. Warriner had a genius for his station as a landlord, and a dignity with it. When the citizens of Springfield gave a dinner to Lord Ashburton, the negotiator of the boundary treaty, it was a superb one; and some days after, one of the leading citizens of Springfield (George Bliss) requested the bill. "I have none," said the host; "I wanted to show Lord Ashburton what Mrs. Warriner *could* do!"

My readers will forgive this parenthesis. In the train of the really great men of the earth there travels the variety of collateral incidents and illustrations, even as the mixed multitude went up from Egypt with the people; and General Washington is a stately subject, which will bear a little side-sketching as a relief. The General was not, by all men, eulogized as deeply as the one great, universal heart of the nation now abides by him. " I am tired," said John Adams, in later life, " of hearing the American Revolution attributed to one man."

Washington took no such honor to himself; but all other names must find their places beneath his own ; how far beneath, is of the questions that the historian, who writes by all the light of years yet in advance, will determine. It is sufficient for us to revel, in our day, in the exultation how pure and grand a man was the central figure of our early history. We might lose all else, but be historically rich in him.

It has seemed to me a little curious that, visited as he was at Mount Vernon, after his presidency, by all varieties of men, there is so little trace, in books of travel or reminiscence, of his conversation. His deeds, not his words, make his biography. Doubtless he was an exceedingly careful man,— more careful in the expression of his opinions than was Mrs. Washington. The attacks which press and party made — yes, made even on George

Washington — annoyed her, irritated her greatly. They grieved the General; and he, I believe, thought that if republics could be thus ungrateful, it might be a forerunner of decay.

Mrs. Washington came in, one cold morning, to her parlor. The General was absent. His orders were to be economical of the wood, that he might impress his neighbors with a sense of the value of its preservation in the policy of farming. The room was chilled, and she rung vigorously for the servant, who came, and she ordered a liberal supply of wood for the fire. The servant excused the condition of the room in the orders of the General. She, after a time, sent again for wood, and when the General returned, there was a rousing blaze. " I am glad," said he, mildly, as he looked at the glittering hearth, " that you have made it so comfortable; but, my dear, we must recollect the example of economy we have to show to our friends around us." Madame, quickly and rather tartly, answered, " If General Washington wishes to see how much his example is cared for by the people, let him read the opposition newspapers ! "

It is possible I may have prejudice against that distinguished lady, but it has always seemed to me that an analysis of the circumstances of his last sickness will show that, if she had risen when he first indicated to her his disturbed breathing, instead of lying comfortably quiet till morning, Dr. Craik might have found a disease more yielding to his medicine. Besides, her will seems to me to be formed on opposite principles from that of her husband, and, in the instance to which I refer, seemingly in contradiction.

Very carefully the librarian of the Boston Athenæum preserves in a side room, and quite on upper shelves, covered by a grating of a very watchful appearance, the books that formed a portion of the library of Washington. And there is need of this care. Melancholy it is to be compelled to suspect that there might come up even these broad staircases, and in these spacious halls, and in these elegant apartments, those who would not merely treasure up the recollections of this precious collection, but, advancing from the mental to the physical, would carry off something more than a memory — a volume or two. Such outrageous spoliations have many precedents, and are not mythical alarms only.

There have been remarkable, perhaps illustrious, appropriations of the rare and beautiful. In the Crimean campaign, the Zouaves declared that they " borrowed " what they took. Napoleon taught some rare paintings and statuary the road to Paris and the Louvre. Marshal Soult was known to have

adorned the walls of his house by mastering some
works of the old masters ; while secretly and with
covert act and stratagem, the plot to steal the very
bones of Whitefield, from his tomb beneath the New-
buryport pulpit, was almost a success ; and even
the grave at Mount Vernon was threatened.   So
the Athenæum at Boston did well to institute guard
over these precious books.   Caution is advisable
in relation to that department of mankind, always
described in the programme of a patriotic procession as " citizens and strangers."

Of exceeding interest are these volumes, and
chiefest those associated with his earliest years.
They illustrate the grave, firm, decent, practical
boy, the coming man.   They show the forming
purposes of the wise, calm, steadfast, true-hearted
republican.   It was only by a special effort that
these books were preserved to America.   Some
gentlemen in Boston heard of the extraordinary
fact that they were about to be purchased for the
British Museum, and they roused to this peril of a
national disgrace.

There was one which I examined, a curious
book, and which should, by a reprint, be in all our
libraries.   Its title is

"SHORT DISCOURSES UPON THE WHOLE COM-
MON PRAYER.   Abridged to inform the Judgment
and excite the Devotion of such as daily use the same."

It was published at the Middle Temple Gate, in
Fleet Street, 1712, and is commended to the pervading loyalty, on both sides of the water, of that
day, by its dedication to the most noble and high-
born Princess Anne of Denmark. It has for us a
better and a loftier dedication. Upon its cover
leaves, Washington essayed his skill in chirography; and it is characteristic of the deference and
filial respect of his young years, that it is the name
of his father that he writes there, over and over.
His father, Augustine, has himself written his own
name in the title-page, and it is a very indifferent
and commonplace writing; utterly different from
that neat, strong, elaborate signature, which is so
appropriately that of his illustrious child. The
boy George experimented largely on his father's
name; and this book of common prayer could not
have gone far astray as long as these leaves remained.

The very writing the boy made contained a
prophecy, of which he did not dream. Yes

"He builded better than he knew."

In a bold and handsome inscription, he has written
August Washington. It was, in his act, the abbre-
viation of his father's name; but the voice of a
world's judgment declares it the appellation be-
longing to himself.

There is another book, which it is interesting to examine. It is a watchword to one of his great pages of duty. Its title is, " Inquiry into the Art of War;" and it receives its dedication to a man, at whose name, less than a hundred years since, Boston's very heart called out to mutiny, — John, Earl of Bute. It is the compilation of Charles De Valiere. Was he kindred to the lovely woman, who, we are told, did what so few of the beautiful of the court of France ever did, — retraced her steps from evil to good ?

Its opening sentence is a curious one, and one which Washington never believed, —

" Honor is a vague expression."

There are volumes upon husbandry, which indicate that the farm at Mount Vernon found the brave soldier and the unsullied statesman prepared for the arts of peace, as well as for the conflicts of camp and cabinet.

In one of the pages he wrote the name of his mother ; and one of his own signatures resembles the style of those quaint, complicated, and ornamental deeds of conveyance, which form the curiosities of the pen-work of the past.

We imperfectly estimate the manner and bearing of Washington by casting it in the mould of our own times. Even in the old-world countries, there is no longer any awful reverence surrounding monarchy itself; and as for the titled, they must show something of mind or great opulence, or they are in danger of being confused with the crowd. It has been my judgment, that with General Washington, after the cloud of party feeling had begun to rise and veil somewhat the enthusiastic days of the Revolution and the thoughtful ones of the Constitution's creation, the belief in the full efficiency of the republic measurably waned. Years after Washington died, the greatest man of his cabinet, Alexander Hamilton (it was in 1804, I think), expressed to Mr. Quincy the belief that the republic would not last forty years. (There were a few days in the year that marked that period — 1844 — when some of us thought his predicting not distant from the actual condition of things.) Washington had established in his mind the truth, that, to the mass of men, the form in which a principle is cast is of as much or more weight than the principle itself. He knew, as all men who observe the continuous history of mankind know, because the facts of a thousand years of civilization force the knowledge on us, that he who rules for the greatest good of all must rule strongly and rule at a distance. He was little less annoyed by the views of some who surrounded Mr. Jefferson than he had been by the oppressive policy of

3

Lord North. Just at that time, France acted in a way that made all men regret to find that its illumination was but the prelude to a conflagration ; that the sword, which had been unsheathed with the pretence and perhaps the purpose to free men, had chiefly employed itself in murdering them.

And so Washington became a man of form, of personal dignity, of state, not so much in its ornaments, for above all that his soul rose, but in its cold, calm isolation.

We are every day becoming more anxious to know which of all portraits and statues of Washington is *nearest the truth*, which best presents to us the man as he actually was; for this, beyond all genius of idealization or wasting of coloring, is the value of a portraiture, and the worth of a genuine original is a very practical affair. Only a brief time since, I found the intelligent president of the New York Historical Society examining authorities at the State Library, respecting the verification of a portrait, whose value, if established, was available at thousands of dollars. It will be interesting to know Mr. Edward Everett's criticism on the justly famous Houdon statue. He says, in a letter to me, " Its 'merits I have ever thought very great. I own I think the fasces out of proportion to the rest of the work, and, considering that Washington was a private citizen when the statue was modelled (1785), of doubtful propriety. The person is stated to have been modelled from life ; in that case, Washington must have considerably increased at a later period, which was no doubt true. Viewed by itself, and without the head, owing to the tight fit of the clothes, it does not give an idea of the traditionary grandeur of Washington's form. In other words, precisely the same objection may be made to it which is made to Powers' statue of Webster."

Perhaps our own state (New York), in its new capitol, will yet place that statue of Washington which, made by the most eminent of sculptors, shall, avoiding all idealization, and drawing its truth from 'all sources, be, in all respects, the most real resemblance that, in marble, can be made of man.

Of Franklin, I found only one man, among aged citizens, who had reminiscence of him, and that was the delightful Quaker, or Friend, Isaac T. Hopper, who seemed to me a man very earnest in the fact and very lovely in the manner, of doing good. He recollected to have seen Franklin in the streets of Philadelphia, and to have received a very kind word of salutation and encouragement even in this passing street inter-view. The last time that he saw him was in a

sedan chair, on his way to the state-house. It is
very singular to me that more was not made, by
historians, of his participation in the great Union
Albany Convention of 1764, especially by Albany
annalists; but I do not recollect of ever having
heard any reminiscence of it from the old gentlemen of that city. It was held, I think, in the old
court-house, or city hall, which stood at the south-
east corner of Hudson street and Broadway (then
Court street, afterward South Market street); but
of the grand old philosopher's action, as a visitor
to that ancient city, I can find no trace. It is
easy to suppose that he enjoyed the hospitalities of
the leading families and official people, because he
was known already as a man of mark; but a convention so important, where such a man was
a master-spirit, and where crown and colony and
tribe had representation, deserved a minute chronicle.

It is an incident, I think, not generally known,
that, after the war, Franklin proposed to Washington that they should visit Europe together. What
travellers! To our eyes, looking through history,
it would seem that it would have been the occasion for a series of ovations; yet the men were
very differently viewed in Europe. To have secured, each, the highest order of welcome, the one
should have gone to France, the other to England,

Wisest, the General decided that he could not leave his home.

Mr. Jefferson's life lasted so far into our own time that he seems close to us. A man he was of a grandeur of intellect which made him a master of his circle wherever he went. Mr. Henry S. Randall, his historian, his best historian, and the one in whose labors Mr. Jefferson's family have expressed their high approbation, told me that his researches did not confirm the current idea that there was dissension between him and Washington; and this may be so, yet I think it is proved that he believed that the General had not the same idea of the essential development of republicanism which he possessed, which his French life had strengthened. What vast suffering to this country might have been obviated, if Mr. Jefferson had been at home, in the Philadelphia constitutional convention, instead of in his diplomatic duty! We think of him as a radical. I suspect he was a very guarded one. He, by no means, satisfied Citizen Genet. He had a manner that was irresistible. Mr. Verplanck says, that when Van Polanen, the minister from the Netherlands to our government in the days of Washington went to make his official first call— his presentation — it was with great ceremony. The Secretary of State arranged and appointed the precise hour, and, at that exact hour, the awed Netherlander arrived, and the folding-doors were opened, and the General stood in the centre of the room, an embodiment of potential presence ; and this suited Mr. Van Polanen and he went away from the interview delighted. He could feel like bringing the ancient name of the house of Orange before such a man.

After a successful diplomatic service, he returned home, probably delighting the dinner-tables of Amsterdam by his recitals of the grandeur of the great American. As he had behaved well, the Netherlands, knowing that great lesson in the conduct of human affairs, when they were well served, after nine years sent him again to this country. Mr. Jefferson was then the President. Remembering the former etiquette, Mr. Van Polanen applied to the Secretary of State, Mr. Madison, as to the day and hour when Mr. Jefferson would be pleased to receive him. "I think he will see you now," said Mr. Madison to the surprised diplomat, who expected a future interview. Mr. Madison called for a carriage, and went immediately up to the President's house, and without delay or doubt presented the minister immediately to Mr. Jefferson, who, as they entered, was seated near the chimney-piece, in a manner especially unstudied. Conversation ensued, and Mr. Jefferson's power was soon displayed ; for the Hollander, accustomed and prepossessed as he was in form and ceremony of court, declared as he left him, that he was "just as much pleased as when I saw General Washington."

No ordinary man could have successfully met the ordeal of this comparison. But this was in Mr. Jefferson, and such is the testimony given me by Mr. Hale, the author of a History of the United States, who numbered among the most fortunate incidents of his life that he made a visit to Monticello.

Mr. Jefferson welcomed him, scarcely noticing his letters of introduction, and at once made his arrangements for the day, telling him that he claimed an hour and a half for his exercise on horseback, and at all other times proposed to be interesting to his guest. He conversed fully, freely, but always as if pronouncing judgment on men and affairs, formed after mature deliberation, and not admitting of contradiction ; an air and way of becoming authority, in him entirely appropriate. His powers of conversation were especially fascinating to young men. Mr. Clay spoke approvingly of Jefferson's conversation, and slightingly concerning Madison in that line.

Certainly he had that in him which made men proud of any association with him. A veteran politician, John Cramer, said to me, " When I was

twenty-four years of age, I held the proudest office
I ever held or ever expect to hold, — I was an
elector for Thomas Jefferson.

Ex-President Tyler declared him to be the most
charming talker he ever knew, — that he never disputed, except with philosophers, but yet always
gave his opinion as fixed and settled.

Who can ever forget the profound sensation
which the news of Mr. Jefferson's death, occurring
on the 4th of July, 1826, occasioned in the Northern States, when its announcement increased the
interest and feeling already produced by the sooner
received tidings that on the same day of festive
celebration John Adams had died? It was not
that these distinguished men had both left earth on
the Independence Day, but that they, above all
men, had been most associated in all our history
with it. As an event involving great coincidence
of extraordinary circumstance, it swayed the public mind to a degree which was absorbing. It
seemed to canonize the whole affair of the Revolution, and it was theme of voice and text of pen for
the nation; and this feeling was in degree renewed
when nine years afterward James Monroe died on
the same day.

Mr. Monroe's own name has been obscured in
the fact which ought to have been considered one
of the chief claims to most honorable distinction,

that in his day of the chief-magistracy, party
slept, and men fraternized, resting from the strug-
gles of the past, and preparing for the long, long
contests of the future. Mr. Monroe was a great
man in the variety of his public service, if not else.
He had seen every department of trust and honor
in civil, diplomatic, and military life, and he came
to the presidency — an eight years' presidency —
by an easy progression. He seemed to be lost in his
old age in the crowds of New York; all we heard
was that Mr. Gouverneur was postmaster because
he was of Mr. Monroe's family, and this seemed
a very proper arrangement. The city realized its
citizenship of a man so distinguished most when
the funeral gun sounded to express a nation's
honor over his grave. And yet a living authority
says to me, " Monroe was only a good, top-booted
man, — himself nothing, his cabinet everything."

Of Lafayette, I can write from personal recollection. That he was to come at all, that he was
a living man to come again among us, the Lafayette of the Revolution, seemed to us, in 1824, of
the strangest ; for he certainly appeared to us, who
were as boys to see him, as already in the pan-
theon of history ; and the idea that we should
make personal acquaintance with one of the greatest of revolutionary names gave to the promise of
his coming a romantic and unreal interest. All

that I saw of him was at Albany, where we were all, old and young, in a delicious excitement about it. The pleasantest narrative of his coming to New York, of his arrival in this country, is in Mr. Cooper's Homeward Bound. We all remembered the name of the Cadmus packet; and that ship thenceforward bore a charmed designation. He was to come to Albany by the James Kent steamboat, — the best and largest of all the old fleet; the one, I remember, in which it was made a mighty effort to accomplish the passage from New York to Albany in twelve hours. He was due by the early afternoon, and all Albany and all Albany's surroundings gathered in high holiday. It must be remembered that Lafayette was a very reasonable foundation for a vivid romantic feeling. He had not come in the decorous respectability of the forsaking of farm and warehouse to join the army of the revolution, impelled by the desire to win out a free government for one's own land; but he had leaped into the field and to the side of Washington in a way that would have been rather brilliant in the best days of chivalry. He had come, when a boy, from all that could detain a boy at home, — come in a journey, which, in this day, it would puzzle us to find any part of the earth so far off, — and we expected that day to see that boy. It pushed for us, who took that view of the case, the clock of time the half century backward. There was need of our enthusiasm. It was wanted to give full endowment to our patience. The afternoon waned; and the Point refused to show the great pipe quadrate of the Kent darkening around it.

Mr. Morse and Professor Henry about that day were bright young men, but not bright enough to read the horoscope of their own great discourses. No telegraph could relieve us. Not at a very distant period from that, the same James Kent *did* use a signal to relieve another great coming of the Albany people. It was when everybody was anxious to know whether Eclipse or Sir Henry, North or South, had won the great race; and when it was agreed that the Kent should float a white flag if our northern horse had triumphed, and the white flag was enthusiastically welcomed when it showed itself.

But the crowd that had gathered to see the revolution come back again, — for so Lafayette's coming seemed to be, — though they were faint, were not despairing. Windows were thronged; and all the long line of Market street showed an anxious people, to whom the event was one that fatigue could not thrust aside. At last, as the evening drew near, we were relieved by learning that he had arrived at Greenbush, where there were very good reasons that he should wait a brief season, as there was a tent and a very pleasant company of Visschers and Van Rensselaers and Whitbecks and DeWitts, neighbors of the Edmund C. Genet, whose evening hours of life were peacefully passed in that neighborhood, and who as acutely represented the extreme of the French revolutionary period, as did Lafayette its conservative side. There was a legend in that tent, — " The boy *did* escape." It was the clever thought of William H. DeWitt and of Albany thus to make allusion to the incident when Lord . Cornwallis believed that he had effectually surrounded the young soldier, and expressed himself that the boy could not escape him. And the old man looked pleasantly on this remembrance of one of the perilous passages of his soldier life.

But while the clever words and abundant cheer of the tent at Greenbush kept him from Albany, the shadows of the evening darkened. A few of the people had gone off despairing, and it seemed as if the keenness of the Albany reception was blunted. But when he did cross the ferry, and we had him safe on the shore of the old city he remembered so well, our fathers made the air vivid with their welcome. He was placed safely in the Visscher carriage, with the venerable Stephen Lush, a man of the Revolution, by his side. I

have said, " the Visscher carriage ; " for it seems
ludicrous to us now, in these days of all the opulent variety of equipage, that, as late as 1824, it
was necessary to go over to the ancient house of
the Visschers to find a suitable carriage for the
nation's guest. Yet it was so; and I recollect
well about the preliminary examination and polish-
ing it had at the establishment of Mr. Gould ; for
it was an old vehicle, long put away, and there
was need of new garniture, and the fishes with
which it was flecked needed brightening, and it
had a long preparation for its honors. Up South
Market street, amidst improvised illumination and
beneath green arches, and in the companionship of
a most enthusiastic crowd, the General came ; and
yet, in many instances, comparatively unnoticed,
for his hair (or wig) was dark, and the Mr. Lush
by his side, with his white locks, received the concentrated gaze ; for who could imagine the Revolution coming back to us but with all the incidents
of venerable age. This dark-haired man could
not be Lafayette. We could see faces but imperfectly by the partial light, and hence the crowd
cheered that white head. But Lafayette made all
the acknowledgments ; for he *never* forgot his part.

I stood to see him, just where, in 1860, I stood
to see a pageant procession, in some respects like
this, of the entrance of the Prince of Wales.

The latter receiving a kindness which did our nation so much honor that it evidenced toward the reigning family of our old home almost a revival of a period precedent to that of the Revolution, — the day of loyalty, as that word was understood prior to 1776.

The General was safely sheltered that evening in civic hospitality, and we all went home satisfied. We had seen Lafayette. Henceforth there was a touch of the Revolution about us. The next day, we, that is, the juveniles, concluded that it was our chief and primary duty to watch and record every movement of the illustrious man, and that the demands of education upon us might be postponed. We builded better than we knew. There was more real education in the incidents of those days than in a hundred pages of written history. So, wherever he moved, did we. Just where the city flagstaff now is, at the centre of the large space at the junction of State street and Broadway, was a pump. It might be designated as *the* town-pump, and was worthy of having been the subject of Hawthorne's delightful essay. What quaint superstitions attached themselves to boyish intercourse in that day! Is there yet any of this remaining, or has it all died, in our bright and busy practicalism? We were taught to believe that if, by the side of

that pump, any of us should lie down and count
the stars above us, death would immediately ensue.
I do not know that we precisely believed this, but
the experiment was not made. Perhaps Albany
considered that pump a choice ornament; at all
events, in the day of Lafayette's visit, it was made
the *locale* of a bold but entirely successful homage to our guest. Indeed, it was quite in the style
of some of the incidents that graced Queen Eliza-
beth's progress at Kenilworth.

"There's a bower of roses in Bendamere's
stream," sings Moore, in one of his sweetest songs.
Not quite of roses, but of verdure very profuse and
deep, was there a bower formed and woven around
this pump, and it was indeed a green spot in the
stony Sahara of the city. Upon its top stood a
living eagle, the very bird and emblem of our
nation,— no taxidermist's effigy, but in real life.
Certainly it was a most successful device, but its
full triumph was not in the mere look of the thing.
As Shakspeare, or Sheridan, recommends above
all things, to the players, action, so was this to be
conducted. As, the next day, the General, in his
progress through the city, passed this bower, at
the very moment of his nearest approach to it, up
rose the eagle, and, raising his wings, seemed
about to depart on the glad mission of communi-
cating the tidings that Lafayette was among us.

And I do not doubt that the General thought it a very pretty occurrence, and his suite, a very remarkable one, and to the crowd that followed his carriage a most curious coincidence, that, at that very moment, the eagle should so appropriately rise; but for us, — we who had, in some way only possible to boys, the confidence of the penetralia,— we knew that, at that time, the eagle could not help rising, for he was most uncomfortably pushed thereunto by a dexterous but unrelenting man in the concealment of the bower. The world outside did not know it, and it is type of too many of the instances where the eagle rises, and the showman thrusts, and the crowd shout, and history makes grave record, and only the few know what it was that really made the great occasion.

We, a great multitude of men, women, and children, accompanied him to Troy, whose citizens were profuse in their hospitalities. He went up in a small packet-boat, on the canal; and by the side of his flotilla, on both banks of the canal, this crowd went on, of course, with all the gay and hearty incidents of the clever pleasantries of everybody's contribution to the general exultation. Even now I recollect the ease with which the five miles were walked; and it has always been to me an explanation of the long marches of armies, for the labor seems divided among all, and its individuality lessened. He was received at the Watervliet arsenal, by a salute, that was the most interesting incident of the affair, and the arrangement of which indicated a taste for the dramatic that is .not always found in our people. The old trophy guns, *taken at Yorktown*, were brought out, and we all came to the arsenal, by the side of Lafayette, on the sound of Yorktown's cannon. This incident made all fatigue forgotten. There could be no fictitious enthusiasm about this.

When he left for New York, his carriage, closed, went through the length of South Market street (Broadway), and the lights of a quick and sudden illumination, flashing from door and window, and ranged along the roadway in all the devices of the moment, showed him how keenly the people of Albany grasped every opportunity to do him honor. Like a true-hearted gentleman and man of infinite tact, as he was, as he always was, he insisted on taking the same route again immediately, *with his carriage open;* and the people appreciated this. At midnight, we saw him on board the little black steamboat Bolivar, at · the foot of Lydius street, and Albany felt its page of revolutionary gratitude well and wisely written.

But I have thus far rather delineated his prog-

4

ress than described the individual. Whether the
portrait has grown into my recollections, or that it
is as I think it, Inman's picture of him, which is
the ornament of the governor's room in the capitol, it seems to me a precise likeness. Observing
him, very closely, and knowing at the time the
value of such minute observation, his features have
lingered in memory. He did not seem like a man
of great presence, but of great amiability, of a
gentle and rather benevolent and fatherly look ; not
over mannered, but especially disposed to be courteous to every one. He had a minute recollection
of local circumstances. It was thought that he
had greater tact in self-possession and for ascer-
taining at the moment by surrounding circumstances what he should remember. This is of itself
a very rare talent ; but he had more than this.
He really remembered incidents which were almost
trivial. He recalled, in passing through North
Pearl street, a curious knocker on a door. It was
a brass lion hanging by its hind legs. And in a
conversation with the mother of Solomon Van
Rensselaer, — a brave soldier of Wayne's army and
of Queenston, — he recollected what she had forgotten, that, preparing him for the rigors of a winter
march from Albany to Schenectady ! she had knit
for him a pair of very long and very comfortable
stockings. While his tact enabled him to derive

information that he wished to use, he had these
pleasant memories copiously. He seemed to understand the Americans, — discriminating between
the practical solidity ' of our multitudes and the
spasmodic impulses of the. French mob, whose hor-
rors he had witnessed. It is this that has made
Lafayette such a favorite in our country, and
kept him from his proper place in the estimation of
European historians.

Annoyed and bored he must have been in the
endless demands made upon him by all varieties of
people; but he took it with amazing patience and
cleverness. He found, and his coming drew out
from their retirement, the aged men, — those of
his own years, who like himself had survived the
times, and to all of whom his name had been a
very watchword. *They* felt his coming like a re-
newal of their youth; and he was in continual admiration at the growth of the country he had
known but in its struggle. So both parties and
all parties were very much pleased; and for once
in our national life, from president to populace, we
all agreed. In the pillars of the portico of the
capitol at Albany there are midway some irons
inserted, the use of which has often puzzled the
observer. They supported a temporary balcony,
which was thronged as he came up the avenue,
and from which the attempt was made to drop a

coronal of flowers on his head, — how successfully
I do not recollect. It was a dangerous experiment to any hero who wore a wig, but I suppose all that was thought about. The best of all
about Lafayette's visit, was the healthy, honest,
good heart of the people, who, without affectation
or sycophancy, remembered that a man really
great by service to them, — very great by circumstance, — who had been with and of the best and
greatest of human affairs, was before them, with
them ; and they said, this is all just right, and we
give our whole heart to it. I never heard him
utter a word, being only a spectator from some
vantage ground of post or piazza; but I recollect
that I cherished a smile he bestowed when at
Greenbush, on his way to the Eastern States.
The incident in itself is trivial, but not so as typing
the general love of a whole people.

CHAPTER II.

LEXANDER HAMILTON'S family claim that he was the friend and counsellor and adviser of Washington to an extent and with a daily reliance which the public mind is not yet prepared altogether to hear. If it is so, it is the greatest of praise. Whether it is so in such full extent, is of the controversies of history that may perhaps be strangely settled by the production of unlooked for vouchers in correspondence. As long as I can recollect, his was one of the greatest of all the names of which in the estimate of the highest men in our history we oftenest heard. Mr. Van Buren when first in England, met — for they were then living — many of the old men of the government, or who had had place in it, and all concurred in considering as the greatest man of our country, Alexander Hamilton. To that degree of estimation, party feeling did not allow our people to advance ; but there is, as I write, a vague universality

(53)

of judgment that he saw and could have best provided for, all the coming exigences of our nation.

Talleyrand said that the three greatest minds he had ever known were those of Napoleon and Fox and Hamilton. My associations were those in the sphere of his powers as a lawyer, and these seem to have most forcibly impressed those men who heard him. Levi Palmer speaks of his extraordinary powers of satire, so bright and keen. I have before me some of his legal memoranda, made with the utmost neatness and precision, and in exactness of handwriting.

" PRESUMPTIONS. — A grant may be presumed from length of time. Doctrine at large in Loft's Reports, p. 576 to 593. 2 Vesey 621 intimates the same principle. 12 Coke. St. John *v.* Dean of Gloucester, original lease proved, long possession proved; mesne assignment shall be presumed."

John Woodworth said that Richard Morrison, Abraham Van Vechten, and Chancellor Livingston were the great lawyers of his memory, but that Hamilton was the greatest of men.

I talked with a gentleman who had most interesting and complete recollections of him — of him, he said, whose utterance was of that sweetest and most fascinating eloquence which so seldom, so very seldom, is poured from man's lips. He was standing close beside him when he (Hamilton) was about to begin his great effort in the famous Croswell libel argument, that celebrated case of our judicial record.. The papers of the distinguished counsel had become slightly disarranged, and he looked round for a pin to fasten them, and my narrator having handed him one, the slight courtesy was immediately acknowledged by a bow of accustomed grace,— the gratitude of the true gentleman for every kindness, never forgotten, although at the instant one of the greatest arguments of his life was to be uttered, and his hand was shaking in tremulous agitation.

That dark and bloody man, the Cain of our times, who deprived America of Hamilton, lived his probation out so long among us, that there are living memories of Aaron Burr. He was always to me a very remarkable and impressive man. I recollect being in a coach with him from Troy to Albany, while the eastern section of the Erie Canal was in construction, and that I was fascinated by the pleasant manner in which he talked to me of that which he supposed would, as a boy, interest me, and that I was quite pleased with myself that, when he asked me what other large canal there was in the world, I could promptly give him the answer,— the canal of Languedoc. The impression of his urbanity of manner is indelible. I often saw him, for he lingered about the courts at Albany, as far as I could see, very

much isolated, and with a sort of neglect, or defiance, of his fellow-men. ˙ In his appearance he
was just like the portraits of the French worthies
of the revolutionary period, and was quite unlike
the gentlemen of the time. ˋ I noticed him, while
he was driving a gig through North Pearl Street
in Albany, in the almost paralyzed stiffness with
which he sat upright. Nobody insulted him, and
nobody noticed him intensely, but all men observed him. He attended one of Dr. Beck's
chemical lectures, in the basement-room of the
Albany academy, having with him the Misses
Eden, to whom, I think, he was a guardian in
chancery, and who quite divided our gaze with
him, for they wore the upright collar and black
silk neckerchief which seemed of man's costume.
He has been described to me, by one who was for
many years a law student in his office, as a man
of little originality, but of great and unscrupulous
power of adaptation of the labors of others; of un-
flinching personal courage ; of no conscience, and
despising or ˉridiculing the profession of it in other
men ; of no liberality, except in respect to that
which ministered directly to self. To old men, he
was morose ; to young men, bland and insinuating.
Judge Nelson related to me his having once found
him writing a letter of condolence to some lady, on
the death of her relative, and of the manner in

which, when using in it some appropriate text of
Scripture, he would laugh at his own use of it.

Yet he must have been a good lawyer. Levi
Palmer, who was a strong federalist, and therefore
not prejudiced toward Burr, declares that he kept
the attention of the audience completely enchained.
I have heard a lady speak of the manner in which
Burr talked to her (and she was horrified) of the
tactics which a lady ought to use to her lover, if
she wished him to declare himself; how he should
be driven to it by her apparent reception with
favor of somebody else's addresses. He was, so
Joshua Spencer said, very interesting in conversation, — very cautious in the expression of opinion
about the living.

Burr had a dexterous friend in Matthew L.
Davis, for no one could have written a more ingenious biography — making prominent the kind
and tender traits which he displayed in his correspondence with his bright daughter, Theodosia
Alston; and while thus showing him in a fair light,
not shocking the reader by any indiscriminate ex-
tenuation. It was his best defence ; and yet all the
biographies, real or invented, cannot make for
Colonel Burr any higher place in history than that
of a bad, great man, unnecessarily and obtrusively
bad. It is well known that his was of the few
voices in this country that denied to General

Washington his full plaudit. He remembered that
when the mission to France was to be filled, the
General said, " I will *not* send Colonel Burr ; I
will send, if you wish it, Colonel Monroe."

But Aaron Burr was not a man for our people.
His ideas were of self, and that self was to be
propitiated by whatever, in power or in pleasure,
ministered to it. Yet, all the while, he had the
intellectual justice to see the state of affairs as they
were, and he could not go as far in his individuality as his will, rather than his judgment, impelled ; so, I fancy, he lived, in reality, a very unhappy life, and was, in all his seeming recklessness,
a man who was always warring in his own mind,
and this found unsatisfactory outlet in the sarcasms
and enmities which he had for others ; and yet he
bore himself bravely. It *is* something to withstand a whole people and the popular opinion of
thirty years of obloquy.

I turn to a pleasanter though briefer notice of a
man who was recognized by us, not as one of the
great and master men of the Revolution, but as,
from his close association with them, entitled to be
regarded as among the notables of warriors. Indeed, that Colonel Richard Varick had been military secretary to Washington was enough to give
him rank and respect. He deserved all this for
his own admirable qualities, but his associative posi-

tion was his historical value. I saw what, at the time, impressed me as being done after the elegant way which we call, — because it is a far-off simile, and cannot be closely sifted, — the manner of the old school. (I heard a bright voice once express the wish that that school might be reopened.) It was election day in the city of New York; and, attending school there, I went, as of the sights of the day, to the First Ward poll. It was the First Ward when, as yet, dwellings had not left the lower part of Broadway. Colonel Varick, a fine, tall old gentleman, entered the hustings to give his vote. Immediately, as he came in, the three inspectors rose and remained standing. He, at the threshold, took off his hat and advanced, and, with all the grace of a courteous offering and reception, of the ballot, he voted. It was a pleasant scene, and might have reconciled me to some other reminiscences which have occasionally attached themselves to this department of action.

Mr. Varick, like General Gates and General Knox, lived comfortable, after-revolutionary lives. The latter was a citizen of Boston; and his portly form and his soldier ways were of the remarked and remarkable in society till 1806. General Gates was used by Colonel Burr, when he wanted to compose a ticket for the House of Assembly, which, by its personnel, should command a successful suffrage; and he showed his accuracy of judgment. The voters of New York could not resist so much respectability. Who *could* vote against Horatio Gates and George Clinton and Brockholst Livingston and John Broome? If a parenthesis of political incident may be produced here, one would like to know how these dignities behaved themselves under Colonel Burr's lead, while such a superb intellect as that of Elisha Williams was also there.

Before leaving that period of our history, — its most interesting, but of which the truth, by conversational tradition, was only seen by glimpses; for, like most other observers, I realized the value of history only as the witnesses were in the decay of advanced age, — before reluctantly leaving these shadows, there is a name, in relation to which I coveted to know more, much more; for I am strengthened by all examination in the belief that he was of the greatest of men in that department of action to which he gave — indeed, without figure it may be said — all his soul. I refer to George Whitefield, — of all men, since the day of Paul, the most earnest and powerful in the utterance of the gospel. With him, the voice of the gospel was in such human power as it seldom finds given to it. His likeness, or portrait, is before me. A face, not of itself of dignity or of beauty; but

the record of thousands on thousands of witnesses
leaves not a doubt as to his resistless power. Here
he is, with uplifted hand, rotund face, the defect in
his eye plainly visible, his name inscribed beneath,
and its only appendage, his college degree of A. B.
Though in this life they did not understand each
other, and probably felt the pressure of circumstances in severance, yet of them both, well may
Pembroke College be proud to write in her list
such names as Samuel Johnson and George
Whitefield. I allude to this portrait, for it was
his own gift to a clergyman he greatly loved, and
it is treasured as a valuable association. Of course,
it must have been to him an acceptable likeness,
or he would not have brought it to this country
with him, or selected it.

I could trace abundant tradition of the uprising
of the people wherever he went. ' It was well remembered by some that they had been told of
churches so crowded that ladders were put up on
the outside that there might be auditors at the
windows, even at this inconvenience ; and to the
crowds that awaited him, there seemed to be universal testimony.

As he died as early as 1774, the living witnesses
of his career were very few ; yet the Reverend
Doctor Sprague of Albany, who had a delightful
letter from Dr. Sewell of Maine about him, went

with me to see an old lady, Mrs. Johnson,
who then resided on Arbor Hill, in that city.
She entered the room, like an ideal old person,
leaning upon her cane. She well remembered
hearing Mr. Whitefield. It was at Mr. Eliot's
church, at the North End, Boston. He preached
at dawn, just at daybreak, for the convenience of
the working-classes. He had a very powerful, a
vast voice, and it filled the whole building. She
said it sounded like thunder. The church was
crowded; and the discourse interested her very
much, child as she was. It was a great event for·
her to go, and she was prepared for it the night
before. This recollection survived a great number
· of years, and the impression must have been very
strong. Mrs. Moore remembered, that, in New
York, he once preached in a ropewalk, a curiously shaped place for a great crowd's gathering.
In Boston, he preached also on the common, and
his text was that beautiful wish of the psalmist, to
possess the wings of a dove in its flight into rest.
How beautiful must have been *his* utterances on
such a theme !   ·

There is an almost flippant, or, to use a milder
term, a superficial, idea prevalent in some circles of.
opinion, that Whitefield,.though a forcible one, was
yet, a ranter, — extravagance of speech his characteristic, however well done.   A distinguished

man, whose life was commencing just as Whitefield's closed, expressed to me the judgment that
Whitefield so greatly interested the people, because, in America, we had but little else to fill the
desire for excitement. That was a very cold opinion, and I think I could trace its bias. But this
thought is not just to the orator. Bishop White
said Whitefield was the finest reader of the liturgy
he ever heard ; and the testimony of his biographer
is, that he was a man of dignity and of elegance.
Franklin, who labors to show that he did not share
in his religious views, gives witness to his greatness.
It is time that his place in history was acknowledged to be among the most wonderful of men.
He took the weapons of this world and made them
brilliant in the armory of the faith.

Of private men of the revolutionary period,—
quaint, remarkable, interesting men,— the material
is abundant ; but it would make this work too much
a local chronicle of the old city of Albany, were
these materials to be used here. They lingered to
later days, with perhaps more of observation of
the then time, than action in it. There was an old
man by the name of Vedder, a great pedestrian,
who could not sufficiently express his astonishment
that he had lived to see Utica — which to him was
old Fort Schuyler — with lamps in its streets !
This he said over and over again. There were the

men who had been traders in the far North and
West, leading the most adventurous of lives,
treading Indian paths, and identified with Indian
habits ; witnesses of the successive intrigues of
French and English, of colonial and state efforts,
to use temporarily the alliance of the tribes, reck-
less whether the alliance was sooner or later fatal
to the Indian ; for his destruction, they saw, was
but a question of time.   If I depart from the strict
rule of this book for one instance only, to make
a personal allusion, it is to say that the Indians
gave to my father the name of Fairweather.   I
trust it was for an unvarying sunshine of disposition.   One of these traders, Wilhelmus Ryck-
man, — straight and tall, — used to stride through
the streets as if he came out of an old picture, and
as if nothing of to-day attached to him.   I met
only one person who recollected the celebrated
Aunt Schuyler, so admirably biographized by Mrs.
Grant of Laggan (the lady, Scott said was so
" blue " as to be " cerulean ").   This reminiscent
was a charming lady, herself very aged, who lived
at the very house of the scenes of that biography,
and she only recollected the great and unwieldy
size of Madame.

There is a curious and impressive incident about
the burial-place of Madame, which is near her
house, and it could be easily understood how it
confirms and illustrates history.

For a long period before the Revolution, and before its conflicting opinions disturbed society, the family of Mrs. Schuyler, her husband and herself, were at once the respected and the authoritative centre of society. In this phase of affairs, the husband died, and a monument in the little enclosure near the house is the record of his name and excellence. But she, Madame, was in reality far the most important person of the two, as her recognized rank in history proves. As the troubles of the epoch rose, her sympathies, perhaps against her judgment, however moderately expressed, were with the old, and not the revolutionary way of things, and her death occurred just as the crisis was forming. No monument is raised for her. Her grave is by her husband's side, but it has no designation, and the explanation must be that the popular furore would have made it probable that a monument would have been defaced. The reason remained during the Revolution, and after those seven weary years, new pursuits and new persons occupied the attention of kindred. Mrs. Grant's book has made for this name a distinguished place in literature and in history, so that her annals form a bright and interesting chapter in the record of New York, but there is her unmarked grave.

There was an abundance of interesting and doubtful reminiscence among those soldiers of the

5

Revolution who survived to great age. A prominent lawyer, who took active. part in that long
series of ejectment suits which confirmed the titles
to the land which the State of New York gave her
soldiers, declared that they required careful scrutiny in their evidence, for meeting before the
trial, they would agree as to what should be their
testimony! and this was not always a safe reliance.

They retained the habits of the camp, and
roused up into old soldier ways when they thus encountered each other ; but the lawyers of that day
soon understood them, and could at last define the
probabilities out of all the conflict of evidence.

That centenarian clergyman, Dr. Waldo, who
closed, in 1864, a life begun in 1762, told us of a
French soldier, one of our allies, who with his
companion was passing one revolutionary day a
house where a spinning-wheel was in use. He
listened for some time to the humming monotone,
and then offered the spinner some money, saying,
" It is the fashion in my country always to pay for
the music, but this is very poor music."

Cashier Van Zandt related to me that he was
walking on the ramparts of Fort Frederick, State
street, Albany, on the day of the battle of Saratoga, and heard the sound of the cannonade. He
asked a soldier about it, and he told him that the

sound followed the course of the river, and the wind was north-cast.

The same gentlemen gave me a very intelligent and probable account of the actual coming into Albany of General Burgoyne as a prisoner. The popular idea would seem to be that he came in surrounded by a body of his own men, fellow-prisoners, with much of the pomp and circumstance of a martial captivity; but General Schuyler was too much of a gentleman to make a spectacle of a distinguished soldier. Mr. Van Zandt with some other boys was playing at the wharf at the foot of State street, — it was one of the few that Albany then possessed, — and word came, in some of those ways in which boys hear everything, that General Burgoyne was coming down Market street. And so he ran thither, and saw a few gentlemen on horseback, quietly moving southward on their way to General Schuyler's house. One of these was John Burgoyne, and another, the aide-de-camp of his conqueror.

But at one locality in his progress down the street he was interrupted. It was sufficiently rude at the time, but we cannot wisely judge in peace of the rudeness of war. General Burgoyne had made some large declarations of his intentions as to Albany, which was *the* great prize of the upward (Admiral Vaughan) movement, and of his own downward progress; and, among other words, had said he should have " elbow room" at Albany. This was remembered. At the corner of Hudson and Court (now South Broadway) streets, lived a Mrs. Stoffel Lansing, who, as the General was passing, shouted out vociferously, " Elbow room, elbow room for General Burgoyne ! " thereby winning quite a traditional reputation. I can imagine that John Burgoyne, as a man of sense, must often have smiled in his recollection of this incident.

He was a gentleman ; for, in his place in parliament, he stood up and gratefully acknowledged the superb hospitality with which General Schuyler had entertained him and his suite at his house in Albany. So strongly did the reputation of this hospitality abide, that, in 1860, when the Prince of Wales was passing through Albany, Dr. Acland, his physician, declared that nothing but his imperative duties, in attendance on the Prince, withheld him from visiting the mansion where his own ancestor had been so kindly and liberally treated. I wish I had personal reminiscence of the distinguished Schuyler to record ; but strangely, though living in the city of his residence, I do not recollect to have ever heard him made a subject of conversation in any special mention. His house I have examined with the utmost interest.

The very vanes that are on the out-buildings are quaint, and have a reference to the incidents of ruder days.

There was a gentleman who, in old age, is well recollected by me, who had borne, though not a conspicuous general, a national part in the Revolution, and in the northern section of the state, had been of large service. This was John Tayler, whose name was so prominently associated, in the political history of the state, with that of De Witt Clinton, — the one as governor, the other as lieutenant-governor. I recollect seeing a young man under the influence (real or assumed) of the nitrous oxide gas, when such experiments were fashionable, pacing up and down the hall of the academy, exclaiming, " *Vox Populi, vox Dei ;* De Witt Clinton and John Tayler ! " I thought, for his side of politics, he did not seem much out of his way, if he was out of his head. Mr. Tayler had acted as governor when Governor Tompkins was called to the vice-presidency of the United States. While he was lieutenant-governor, he, of course, presided over the senate, and Mr. Verplanck informs us that, on one subject, he was permitted, by the senate, to take part in the debate, which is not, constitutionally, within the province of the lieutenant-governor. Whenever there arose questions concerning the Indians, which, in various

ways, of law or treaty, were abundant, Governor
Tayler would, standing, as it were, by the side of
the senate, rather than in it, give his views,
founded upon his long and eventful experience
among them, and the senate welcomed it as the
word of most valuable counsel. His life took the
period from 1742 to 1829, and he had recollections
of the French war and intimate experiences of the
Revolution. He was one of the party that found
Miss McCrea, murdered in the woods, lying dead,
and observed the tomahawk wound in her breast.
It will be remembered that this was one of the
tragedies of the war, and which was the subject
of severe comment in congress and in parliament.
He knew the Indian character thoroughly, and
was, in that, a formidable rival to the Johnsons,
who, in their life among the Mohawks, presumed
to rule the Iroquois.

The wife of one of the Johnsons was in Albany,
and was more than accused of being a spy on the
actions of the committee of safety. Mr. Tayler
moved that she be requested to leave the city.
" Who will tell her ? " said one at the board, *himself in league with her.* " I will," said Mr. Tayler, with a touch of the old bravery of that Doug-
lass known as Sir Archibald Bell-the-Cat. He did
so. He told her she knew where her husband
was, and he did not. A carriage was sent for her,

and she chose to go to Schenectady. Johnson termed this an affront and insult, and did not forgive it. He sent men, who were fed and lodged in Mr. Tayler's stable, by his colored cook, Chloe, who had been a slave of Johnson, and had been bought by Mr. Tayler, but who remained all devotion to her first master, with a fidelity like that of the clansmen of the Highlands. Mr. Tayler then lived in a house in North Market street (Broadway), near where was the line of defence stockades, and through the grounds of which a creek (Fox) ran to the Hudson river. These men, concealed, were to capture Mr. Tayler. On the night when the seizure was to be made, a slave of Major Popham, an old revolutionary worthy, shut the bedroom window, and was reprimanded by Mr. Tayler. " Master will be taken alive to-night," said she. He instantly understood the warning, and, going to the front window, fired his gun. This was an alarm signal quickly comprehended by the people of the city. Johnson's men also heard it, and they took to their batteau and moved immediately out of the creek to the river, and made their escape. Subsequently it was known that Johnson's order to these men was to take Tayler where he could be delivered to the Mohawk Indians; a destiny which indicated about all that was undesirable. Indeed, this is confirmed by another incident. After the war was over, he found, at a book-stall, the family Bible of the Johnson family. He purchased it, for a half-joe, and ˏsent it to Sir John Johnson, in Canada, saying, in irony, that it was in return for the kindnesses he had shown him in the war. Sir John returned word that, if he- *had* caught him, he would have given him to the Indians; which indicated that Sir John had lost his good manners, with his other losses.

When Burgoyne's army was every hour expected, — when so great was the fear of its coming that some citizens of Albany left the city and went for presumed safety to the hills of Berkshire, — Mr. Tayler was out at his country-house, which was a few miles north of the city, in the probable route of the British army, if it should come as conquerors. While Mr. and Mrs. Tayler were talking about the probable incidents of the march, they saw one of their woman slaves dragging a kid to the well, and, at the same time, wielding a knife. "What are you doing?" was Mrs. Tayler's inquiry. Her answer was, "I am going to kill the goat and throw it in the well, so as to poison the water for the British when they come." "Not so," said Mrs. Tayler. "Come in here and help me set the table." "You are crazy, mistress," the slave exclaimed. Mrs. Tayler told her to put the silver on the table, to put on all the cold meat in the house, and prepare the table in its best. Mr. Tayler now remonstrated ; but said Mrs. Tayler, " When General Burgoyne comes past, he will see that this is a gentleman's house, and that this meal was prepared for him. He will spare the house and all its contents ; while, if we remove our things, the house may be burned."

The Major Popham, referred to in the above notice, was a gentleman, for the sake of whose revolutionary service, the State of New York kept alive a court of Exchequer, of which he was clerk, and whose duties were apparently concentrated in that fact. He lived to a great age, and was accustomed, when about to relate a story, to say to his listener, " Young man, if I have told you this story before, interrupt me at once. You cannot insult me more than by letting me tell you a story twice." This was high good breeding, and not often imitated.

I wish I had worthier memories of that really remarkable man of the tribes, Red Jacket, than that I saw him intoxicated in the street. It was his doom, and he fulfilled his weird. Judge Sackett told me, that when Red Jacket was questioned as to his birthplace, he would answer, " One, two, three, four, above John Harris ; " by which he intended to say, " Four miles above the ferry-house of John Harris," — a famous pioneer of the Cayuga country. Mr. Sackett, with historic zeal, has purchased and owns the ground where this forest orator was born ; and it may one day have a monument.

Of General, or Baron, Steuben, while I never heard incident, I have before me writing of his own, which is interesting ; one, as illustrating his peculiar excellence, which was as disciplinarian, a great master of the situation in military affairs ; and the other, as glimpsing, and that not unpleasantly or unfavorably, into his private life. These papers are darkened and faded with age, but they show that Steuben put down in the written record what he designed, and thus created for himself that high order of reputation which is so peculiarly his own. He drilled and disciplined and planned and arranged, at a time when, and in an army in which, men came to do a great work for their country, with a most miscellaneous idea of going to war, every one for himself.

The first is his detailed statement of the formation of troops from those of the States. It will be observed, that, like many other distinguished gentlemen (and ladies), he does not consider correct orthography as among the exact sciences.

" Formation des trois Brigades.

" Virginie, Marryland, et Pensilvanie pour la compagne presente.

1 Brigade Virginie 730
Seconde Brigade Virg'e 750
1 Brigade Marryland 980
Seconde Brigade Marryland 1050
1 Brigade Pennsilvanie 950
2 Brigade Pennsilvanic 860
En tout 22 Batil dans l'ordre de battaile."

The other is a little gray-colored pass-book. The adage is, that no man is a hero to his valet de chambre. Steuben seems to have been prepared to be, what was perhaps better, a just and correct employer. Veteran and valet have both gone into the dust, while the little pass-book remains to illustrate the private life of a gallant old soldier who did his adopted country good service.

" Louis Wolf est entre dans mon service comme friseur et valet de chambre at Philadelphie, le 1 de Fevrier, 1782.

" Je lui ait promis son entreineur comme valet de chambre et une page de dix dollars par mois. Surquoi il a recue a compte les sommes suivantes. — 43 dollars. 50 dollars. Total 93 dollars."

And to this blended French and English is his signature, " Steuben, " not without those cabalistic flourishes, by which, probably, foreign gentlemen mean so much.

I wish I had known old Donald McDonald bet-

ter: first, because he was, in himself, a rare man,
a true Caxon, whose shop was a sure place to
hear something of that quaint talk which, in less
rapid days than the time in which we now haste
in all things, was the characteristic of the barber;
and next, because he declared that he recollected
Doctor Johnson, as coming into a shop in London,
where he was an apprentice; and it might well
have been so, for McDonald was a man who knew
the worth of man. He claimed to have seen Fox,
and to have been of the Buff and Blue. The
habitués at McDonald's were of the best. men of
his vicinage, and they made memorable hours
there. There might have been interesting Dies
McDonaldienses written. He said, before he came
to Albany, Governor Jay bought his wigs from
London. The last heads he powdered were those
of the Patroon and a Mr. Penfield, of Ontario
county.

I confess pleasant surprise, though nothing about
it ever came within my observation, at finding, in
history, that Flora McDonald, whose name is imperishably associated with Prince Charlie, was
once a resident of our country, and, chased on her
voyage home by one of our privateers, pleasantly
remarked that she had been in danger, as
well for the house of Hanover as for that of
Stuart.

That was a very curious story, related to me by an aged counsellor of New York, whose acquaintance with the city land titles was very minute, that Charles Graham kept a fort, in Garden street, for the Pretender, and only surrendered on condition that he should have the old walls of the fort to build a vault in Trinity church-yard. I should like to believe it, if I could, for it would be a dainty bit of romance to inlay our city map. I have not been able else to find record that our country was at all stirred by " the affair of '45," except finding an address in which, I think, the detested Duke of Cumberland was eulogized.

Probably no one name in all English literature is so universally a ceaseless interest with reading men in this country as is that of Dr. Johnson. We read all of him, or of his associations, with delight. Even the minute record of Boswell did not satiate the world-wide circle of admirers of the man who was the leader of a company of intellects, each one of whom has left a name that adorns letters.

Mrs. Piozzi's book was one of the latest additions to our history of Dr. Johnson, and because of her knowledge of him, it became interesting to learn all that we could know of herself. It will be seen, by reference to her book, that she had, in her extreme old age, a species of absurd sentiment, or flirtation, for Mr. Conway, an actor, with whom she corresponds, and to whom she bequeaths testimonials of affection.

When Gilfert had his magnificent company of actors at Albany,— a set of men whose equals it would be difficult to find in any one gathering of that art in America,— he made a brief engagement for Conway, whose master part was that of Hamlet.   I recollect seeing him, as his service was over, going through the street on his way to the steamboat, and a conversation occurring about the success of his week, which had been quite remunerative.   He was tall and very handsome, and was considered to have all his capital in his good looks, and that his intellectual endowment was a very light one.   If it had been known that he was the pet of the charming Thrale, whose house was Johnson's happy home for so many years, Mr. Conway would have had our stare to all the extent an actor's love of notoriety could have desired.

The tumult of the French revolution sent to our country a large number of refugees, who were of the royalists, or loyalists, to the old government, and who fled to save their heads.   They came, and met the exile with the grace and adaptation to circumstances which puts a Frenchman on his feet all over the world, and which makes them a nation prepared for dominion wherever they go.

These fugitives from the detestable revolutionists were, many of them, gentlemen, and made themselves agreeably known among us by their good manners. They must have been in a great fear of the power they had left behind them, as, in one instance known to me, the individual changed his name, assumed a new one for his passport, and retained the latter in this country, when his descendants, afterward seeking for the old place and name in France, could not find it, but were recognized so soon as they deciphered their former estate. These gentlemen brought with them handsome dress and furniture, saving, as well as they could, something out of the wreck. Their necessities induced them afterward to dispose of these, and I could yet readily find a curious escritoire, very richly and elaborately inlaid, which was said to have come out of the palace, though it is not probable that they who fled from the Tuilleries essayed to save anything but themselves, fortunate if they took their head, in its natural position, away with them. They returned, as many as could go, when the better " order " prevailed again, and others faded away, pleasant and queer, their hearts in the old home. A number of them lived on or near the Hudson and the Mohawk rivers, a few miles northward of Albany; and it was the theme of considerable neighborhood wonder when the child of one of them died and was *buried in its cradle.* Either these old-world men, or the people of other old days of war and adventure, gave something of legend to this neighborhood. In the latter part of the last century, a family whose characteristic would be that of calm good sense, resided in one of the houses near the Hudson river, not far from the Aunt Schuyler house of Mrs. Grant's history. A variety of superstitious stories were rife about the house, and when this family went there to reside, it was confidently told them that they would be disturbed by sights and sounds unearthly.

It held the unenviable reputation of being a "haunted house." The family were not moved by all these stories. They believed they had no other foundation than the imagination of their superstitious Dutch neighbors, and their possession of the premises was undisturbed. I wish to say that what follows is supported by testimony which, in my knowledge of its entire reliability, is irresistible, and the explanation is to this hour in mystery.

One summer *morning near noon,* so that no shadow of night was in the affair to give it uncertainty, the lady of the house with her servant was in the house attending to some domestic duty, when they, *both of them,* saw approaching the house, an elegantly dressed old gentleman, his costume old-fashioned, with short clothes, silver knee-buckles, silver shoe-buckles which glittered in the sun, hand-ruffles, cocked hat, all quite of the distinguished gentleman cast. He seemed coming to enter the house, so that the lady told her servant to remove some obstruction from the hall. Suddenly he disappeared, and they could see nothing of him, nor could they afterward find any trace of him. His coming was right in the way where the master of the house was on his route from the field. He saw nothing of him.

The most distinguished of all who came to America was that statesman of all times, Talleyrand. For a time he boarded at Brooklyn, and I have heard Mrs. Cantine, of Ithaca, who was a fellow-boarder with him at the house of Madame Rosette, speak admiringly of the delightful manner in which he read aloud, but generally was dull with the ladies, even to falling asleep in their company. He was at Albany, and Henry Abel would insist upon it that he had seen him walking out with his violin in amusing himself; but I doubt he mistook some less stately refugee for him. He boarded at the house of Louis Genay, whose sign, L. Genay, was a waif that came down to later times. This Mr. Genay (whose descendants have changed the spelling to Genet), was the sexton of the Roman Catholic Church in its inception at Albany; and

6

when the first mass was said at the house of Mrs. Cassidy, it is tradition that Talleyrand was among those present. The Bishop of Autun! he might have officiated.

Of Le Ray de Chaumont, so well known in our North, and whose name is perpetuated by its association with Lake Ontario, I only recollect that when he travelled to Albany he brought his cook with him; a procedure which, though it showed his care for himself, as he came to the hotel of Leverett Cruttenden, might be considered as adding gilding to the refined gold.

Something of that new First Family of all the earth, the Bonapartes, crossed our horizon. The annual journeys of Joseph from his beautiful River Point palace at Bordentown, to Ballston and Saratoga, were noticed; and I remember that Hermanus Bleecker defended a suit brought by Erastus Young, a coach proprietor, against Joseph, for some alleged breach of contract in the coaching between the Springs and Albany. My sympathies were for the exile, as I knew into what hands he had fallen in this case. The brother of his brother, and ex-king of Spain, I hope was successful. This I know that in Mr. Bleecker he had distinguished counsel and the best of friends.

I have talked with some men who were so fortunate as to see *the* Napoleon, — the man who made

his own fame and left a capital in excess, which at
this day governs a great fraction of the world,
and the celebrity of which does not seem to grow
old. I call these men who thus saw him fortunate
indeed, for the curiosity of history in respect to
him is insatiable, notwithstanding that a Napoleon
library of memoirs would already fill the house.
The great reason why mankind is so entranced
about Napoleon is, that he came from the crowd
upon the old dais of imperial dignity, and had all
the romance of life about him. He blazed, and
our eyes are even yet dazzled by the light. I have
talked with those who saw him in his power, in his
exile, at his grave, — only to look at him, it is true ;
but even of this Beranger makes material for song ;
and one is gratified at some other evidence about
him as he actually was, than what is found in memoirs and biographies, most of which were written
to advance some great theory of government.

Charles King, one of the most agreeable of
men, saw him at a military review, and he sat, not
stolid of course, but as banishing all expression
from his face ; but his horse made some false movement, and in an instant his look was intensely animated and his eye brilliant. Mr. Bayard declared
his smile the sweetest that could be imagined.
He saw the grand departure of the guards for
Austerlitz. It was in all the scenic accompani-

ments of a city's pageantry. It was Mr. Van Rensselear's good fortune to see the emperor drive into the Tuilleries after the return from Moscow, and forty years afterward to see the Napoleon of our own day go forth from Paris to the Italian campaign. These gentlemen, favored indeed, thus caught glimpses of the Emperor in some hours of his career of power. Governor King also alluded to his handsome face, and his power to banish all expression from it.

I met a quiet, unpretending old man, standing by the side of his son, who was a steamboat pilot. He had been a British soldier, and his regiment was stationed at St. Helena, while the emperor was there in exile. He saw him examine and attend to some plants, and was impressed with the sadness of his look. He had planted some flowers for him.

Another, whose father was on the island in the service, was just old enough to recollect that the object of his admiration and wonder while he saw Napoleon buried, was that he was laid out in his " cocked hat ! "

These are all, it may be, trifling recollections; but they are of a man in relation to whose every movement the world has turned with an interest to know all and everything about him. I can recollect what great favor was extended, by the popular opinion in America, to Dr. O'Meara's book, which revealed the ill-treatment of the Governor of St. Helena toward the emperor, and that the feeling in this country was almost in unanimity one of sympathy for the great exile. Then, nothing seemed less likely than a return of the name of Bonaparte to power, except that a lingering hope watched the life of the young Duke of Reichstadt. When he died, the world's hope for " the family " seemed extinguished.

That we should live to see the name of Napoleon one of the ruling ones of the world was outside even of all the romance of history. I believe the peaceable years which followed 1815 had educated mankind to the belief that war was an affair of the past, and that the European world was to go on in the decent dulness of legitimacy. .

Hence, part of the feeling which now gives such prestige to the Napoleon III. is, that his coming to power seems to be a chapter of poetical justice. The Napoleon was exiled, we all believed, in an unjust, unfeeling, and cowardly manner. Such is the impulse of the popular opinion, even though the truth of justice may, or ought to, soften that judgment. To see Napoleon III., by his uncle's name, an Emperor, in the grandeur of his power, is the romance properly written out again.

When Louis Napoleon came to New York, it

was to the City Hotel, kept by Mr. Mather. Colonel Webb and some friends were dining there. Mr. Mather requested permission to bring him into the pleasant circle, as a stranger; and he joined them in an evening not likely to be forgotten. I do not at all believe the stories about any low-life associations formed by him while in New York. On the contrary, he was select and careful as to the invitations that he accepted; and I have heard Mr. Raymond say, that he took pains to ascertain, when in London, whether the accounts which were frequently given of his destitution in that city were true, and he found that they were not; that he lived pleasantly and respectably, and that the chief impression there concerning him was that he was slightly insane; as he, a private gentleman, in the obscurity of the multitude of London, while a great and powerful monarch was apparently in complete power on the throne of France, would often say, and say it seriously, "When I shall be at the head of affairs in France." What could sound more like insanity? And yet he is head of affairs imperially in France, and not very much removed from being head of affairs in England, also.

I think there is to-day a much clearer idea of what Napoleon really was, than in his own time. The world judges best in the distance; at least, such is a maxim in history, and I almost give in

adherence to it. Europe seems to have been surprised and indignant, that the new man should
have been so presumptuous as to invade the old
order of things ; and, in our own country, federalist and democrat persisted in borrowing English
and French spectacles, with which to look at him
and his actions, while they could have seen clearly
through their own just vision. It was a long
series of years before we comprehended that Napoleon was not exactly of the French revolution,
that he was not a partner of the miserable
wretches, who insulted the name of humanity by
their actions, but that he was behind all that trag-
edy, and came on the scene at a later hour. Now,
we understand all that, and judge of him in a fair
estimate of all that he really did ; and the universal American feeling is that of admiration, not so
entirely obscuring our senses but that we see he
was, in its most intense sense, an individualist ; but
he was so on a scale so grand as that it compels
the public heart. I have seen attempts to break
up this enthusiasm ; but it is in vain. A few men
listen to Dr. Channing ; but the great voice of the
people is in the Vive Napoleon. I heard the wise
and venerable Josiah Quincy and his estimable
relative, Mr. Watterston, discuss as to what would
be the one name of that age, if it settled into one
designation ; and, while Mr. Watterston said the

Age of John Howard, the sagacious old man said, the Age of Napoleon.

To this day, without reflecting on consequences, I think there is a strata of disappointment, in the American mind, that the battle of Waterloo resulted as it did ; and that, not because of ill feeling toward England, but because it was out of the rules that Napoleon should know what defeat was.

My readers will think that I linger as long in and about the day of the Revôlution, as if I were of the immortal band of pensioners. It is the shadowy and romantic era of our history. Thenceforth, we get into the broad glow of modern realism, and look at men with little belief in their quaintness ; while, for any of the men, whose lives were, in greatest degree, of the last century, we may take all old ways and customs as of the texture of their lives.   When Timothy Pickering was in his last sickness, as he had never been sick before, the doctor (it seems to me, with more politeness than most doctors show to us) consulted him as to what medicine he would take. " Why," said he, " let me see, the last medicine I took was when I was at Yorktown, fifty-five years ago, and that was glauber salts. I think that will do."

Mr. Quincy told me, that, in his younger days, nothing was more common in the lesser courts of

Boston than to hear John Hancock's name called in default. But he had with that a much pleasanter recollection of him, as having, when a boy, dined with him. The Governor sat at a little table, apart from his guests. A servant, in entering the room, stumbled, and crashing down, came glasses and plates from the epergne. "O John, John," said he, "break as much as you want to, but don't make such a noise." And, in this joke, he forgot the damage to his china.

A few years before the Hancock house was pulled down, I recollect seeing an old gentleman pacing up and down in front of the house, a good representative of the name. It looked like the historic house then; and, I must say, that it was an amazement to men outside of Boston, that *any* money consideration was strong enough to prevent the city of Boston from retaining, as long as stone walls would exist, the Hancock house. Boston came down several degrees in the general thermometer when the demolition of that interesting mansion was known. I confess, the city has looked a little common-place to me since then.

The old river families of New York had not quite lost their caste of influence in my earlier recollection. The Van Rensselaer was a popular name, as represented to us by the old Patroon, in those days a proverb for all that could be supposed opulent; and the respected, quiet old gentleman, with a variety of carriages, with the old fashion of powdered hair, walking at the slow pace of leisure through the streets, always with one hand ungloved, and the very solid fact that his was a domain of estate reaching twelve miles from his manor house in all the four ways of the compass,—all this made him quite one of the personages of the times. It was known that, at his death, the grandeur of his estate was to be diminished, and we heard vague and undefined relations of all that entail had, to that time, done for the estate.

The Clintons had a representative that acknowledged no superior.   Of him, I shall write in other pages.

The Delanceys, before the Revolution, a very powerful family, were not then as well known as now, when we recognize their worth in the estimable diocesan of the name.

The Livingstons, though not relatively in rank as before, stoutly, in various ways, maintained their ascendancy. Edward Livingston, recently so admirably biographized, was the very right-hand man of General Jackson, writing for him, in 1832, a proclamation about the South Carolina difficulties, so intensely federal, that I recollect hearing Mr. Harmanus Bleecker say, that it was more decided in federal doctrine than General

Hamilton would have ventured to utter, and Mr. Bleecker thought that figure exhausted all comparison. Charles L. Livingston, a very able and indolent man, was speaker of the assembly, while Edward P. Livingston, ponderous and rather dignified, was lieutenant-governor, and presided over the senate. So the Livingstons rather sustained themselves.

There was an old colonial family (banished by their espousal of the crown side, instead of that of the republic), in whose annals of romance the tax-payers of New York were interested, and romance and taxes do not often touch their velvet and iron hands together.

Frederick Philipse was the owner of a superb manor. It had a dainty domain over a rich territory, in that part of Westchester county where one relic of him yet remains,— the little, quaint weather-vane which is above the old church of the Tarrytown cemetery. Mr. Irving has made all that locality memorable, in his charming stories of Sleepy Hollow, and he lies in the shadow of the old church himself. In that vane the letters F. P. are curiously traced. I suppose the manor house had all the brilliant associations of colonial hospitality, especially as it was at just such a distance from New York as permitted, even in those days and those roads, frequent journeys. And Miss

Mary Philipse was a young lady who won even tnen the attention and notice of our own Washington, then a handsome young officer in the most loyal service of His Majesty George Third. He visited at the manor house, and he could not resist the fair lady; but duty called him eastward. He was ever a reflecting man, and did not at once declare himself, but left, with a chosen friend, a charge to keep watch and ward over his venture in this fair argosy. He left, I doubt not, reluctantly. Detained at Boston longer than he had hoped, his friend wrote to him to warn him that another was bold to win the fair Philipse. He could not return, and the lady, little conscious what a prize she had lost, accepted the proposals of Captain Morris. A nation's destiny was in the choice of the lovely lady, and we may not now stop to reflect what " might have been," which, Whittier well says, are of all words the saddest.

The storm of the Revolution came. The family of Philipse and Captain Morris were loyal to the crown, and in their great, but perhaps chivalrous, error, the lands of the fair manor of Westchester went to the new state, and bills of attainder were passed, which included the name of Mrs. Morris; very ungallantly, but in the hour of war we do not stop for the gentle amenities of life. It is a fast and fierce philosophy we study then.

There were broad and valuable lands in the adjacent county of Putnam, and these, too, went to the public title, and the State, in process of time, made conveyance to settlers. But, when the fever of war is over, nations grow calm and courteous, and wish to forget many a fact which, in the struggle, they flaunted in the face of mankind. The State, after all, thought it not wise to continue the attainder of the ladies, and it was, so far as Mrs. Morris was concerned, removed; and the shrewd and rising John Jacob Astor bought of her her title to the Putnam county lands. Mrs. Morris lived till 1826, and must often have thought if it would not have been wiser for her to have smiled very decidedly on that modest, but very good-looking, young officer who afterward yielded to the charms of the widow Custis.

Mr. Astor took his title to the courts, and a good and strong litigation was had; and I remember to have seen that very impressive looking counsellor, Abraham Van Vechten, engaged in the trial before the court of errors. Mr. Astor's claim was sustained, and then the State, to remunerate those who had trusted its deeds, issued a public stock, called the Astor stock. It was to the amount of several hundreds of thousands of dollars, and was only finally paid up a very few years since. So New York was long taxed because Washington was not a quick-worded lover.

As the manor life of New York has now almost entirely passed into history, what a clever book might be made of its annals! It would be read as we read romances,— interested in the incidents, and not caring for the exact wisdom of facts that are in the dust of time.

When our authors shall look to their home for their incidents, the chronicles of the Hudson will be found a source which will furnish the most interesting materiale for romance, from the hour when a few adventurous and brave men raised the European flag at the mouth of the creek which the Norwegian afterward identified with his name.

Upon the shores of the Hudson lived Mrs. Montgomery, the long mourning widow of the brave and rash and celebrated hero of the Quebec affair of revolutionary story. I recollect seeing her in Albany about the time of his reinterment, when the State of New York, awaking from a long sleep on the subject, had his remains, in all succession of ceremonial, brought from Quebec, where their first battle grave had been, through line of pageantry and funeral pomp to New York, where, in front of St. Paul's church, the mural tablet is the object that amidst the greatest, loudest confusion of life, fixes the eye of the stranger ; for all over the world

there is a strange fascination in the reading of
epitaphs. Its philosophy is that we seek to know
all we can about the grave in this chapter of its
work, even though we know that affection or respect or something else than the real truth, is the
virtue of all this monumental literature.

Mrs. Montgomery was at Albany at this period,
and what especially impressed her look on my
memory was her extraordinary small eyes, so like
those of a Chinese. The pageant at Albany was
in all the best of pomp that the city could furnish.
At its head rode Major Birdsall of the regular
army ; and the next week we were out to see his
military funeral, — murdered as he had been by
one of his own soldiers.

If the rock at Quebec was, at the time he led up
that most forlorn hope, in the condition in which
it now is, the attempt then to get into the citadel
was of all efforts the most mad. That of Wolfe
seemed an easy affair in comparison with it.
Montgomery's career and death made a memorable
page in the annals of the British Parliament, and
all the great minds of the era were in that debate,
to extenuate or defend or deplore his course.

Looking, some years since, over old legislative papers of the New York Legislature, I found a copy
of the will of General Montgomery, which I
thought was a curious and interesting document.

It used manly, simple, and affectionate language, the very words for a true-hearted man and a brave soldier to utter. His widow, at a very early period after the Revolution, memorialized the Legislature for a grant of land; and the direction given by the General's will to his property to Lady Ranelagh, was used as one of the reasons for urging the grant.

The committee of the legislature — as is the custom with those gentlemen — used very brave and glowing language about the hero. I don't quite see the grant of land, though we may hope, for the credit of our ancestors, that it was given promptly. At all events, the State named a county after him, and even these shadows of public gratitude are something. There is a peculiar passage in the committee's report which gives a light on history: "that at the siege of Quebec, hope was still entertained of an accommodation with Britain." Well may Sir John Russell, in his editing of Fox's letters, speak strongly of the fatuity that actuated England's counsels in the dispute with this country.

His will gives his property to his sister, Lady Ranelagh, saying, " My dear sister's large family wants all I can spare. The ample fortune that my wife (Janet Livingston Montgomery) will succeed to, makes it unnecessary to provide for her in a

manner suitable to her situation in life, and ade
quate to the warm affection I bear her." And
the will contains also this soldier-like utterance :
" Though the hurry of public business and want
of knowledge of the law may render this instrument incorrect, yet I believe my intention is plain.
I hope, therefore, no advantage will be taken of
any inaccuracy."

I recollect a pleasant old gentleman, Mr. Nich
olas Van Rensselaer, who had accompanied Montgomery on the Quebec expedition, who survived in
all the kindly surroundings of a very comfortable
home at Greenbush, opposite Albany, who had
the mental and physical activity to go to Boston
in 1843, when the top-stone of the Bunker Hill
Monument was laid. It was near his house I met
Edward C. Genet, who, — at one time appealed
from Washington to the people, — believing that
the word Revolution was as potential here as in
France, and that, as he represented the revolutionary government, the people of America would do
everything he could ask. His life had been a very
eventful one in its diplomatic service in Old Rus-
sia and for New France. I thought him brusque
and not in the courtly ways of Frenchmen ; but as
' he found fault with me, and he was an old man and
I a boy, he was probably right.

7

CHAPTER III.

 WOULD like very much to have believed in Eleazer Williams' Dauphinate, for I saw him several times, and it would have been a refreshing property in romance to have thought him, the coming-up of the poor, starved, and abused little· regal boy, upon whom those hyenas of the French Revolution lavished their barbarity. But I never had it smoothed to my historical conscience. He certainly *did* look the Bourbon very strikingly. I saw him examining the cabinet collection of portrait medals of all the long line of French kings and emperors, which Louis Napoleon gave to the New York State Library; and he took off his graceful blue cap, and, placing his hand on his large Bourbon forehead, pointed to the medals of the later kings. But the old man did not look like a distinguished man, but like a good old Indian clergyman, as he was; and it was a pity to disturb his pastoral and pastorate by any wild dreams

98

of impossible uprisings into royalty. If Prince de
Joinville did amuse his and the public's curiosity,
it was very cruel unless the prince knew something more than he has told us; and I do not be
lieve that he did. That he might have been a
natural son of Louis would be an explanation
which would make resemblance and exile quite
consistent.

But he was a better than left or right hand son
of monarchs. He answered me, when I asked him
of the locality of his parish, in the old utterance,
" My parish is the world." It was to me a very
interesting meeting which I had with him and a
group of old and quaint St. Regis chiefs, in the
room of Mr. O'Callaghan in the upper story of
the State Hall, surrounded by all that eminent
scholar's histories and historical labors; and when,
in answer to inquiries these men would give the old,
old names to the city or locality where we stood,
and called the Hudson River by a name so far
back that our geographers had faint memory of
it. They were stout and powerful men, but apparently simple-hearted men of the quiet forest life;
and he among them was the superior who directed
them to higher and happier and holier things.

Of the elder Adams, I heard, in Boston, interesting anecdotes; but I think their general impression on my mind was that he did not look as

serenely on all around him, in his latter days, as did his contemporaries, but was a little cynical in expression. He could illustrate a very impressive truth in a quiet way. As when a friend from Boston coming to see him, while at his own house in Quincy, and while there was a controversy existing between him and Mr. Pickering, — "Is it not," said he, "a melancholy sight to see Mr. Pickering and myself sitting up in our coffins, throwing mud at each other?" I know there are Boston people, living at the date when these sketches are written, who could give most piquant record of the grave and gay sayings of this very remarkable man.

Was he as remarkable a man as was his distinguished son, John Quincy Adams? I doubt it. History will, at a period not very remote, remove the political sand from the base of this statue, and it will appear in all its grandeur. I saw him on two occasions; and, in both of them, — though one was but an ordinary occurrence of life, — I was profoundly impressed. I remember well the oration which he delivered in the Middle Dutch Church, in Nassau street, now the post-office, on the occasion of the celebration of the fiftieth anniversary of the adoption, or inauguration, of the constitution of the United States. There was, as may readily be supposed, a great crowd to enjoy this voice of history, by one who had been so much of, and near to, all of it. The crowd especially enjoyed the coming in of Winfield Scott, in all the equipage of his full dress, as head of the army. That great stature and overlooking proportions told admirably on the scenic effect of such an entrance ; and, for a time, the attention of the audience was divided between the orator and the soldier. The discourse Mr. Adams pronounced is of the great documents of our history. His manner was very earnest and commanded attention.

The building in which he spoke was, of itself, a discourse. It had, and yet has, the great walls which our ancestors seemed to have judged necessary to bear a burthen, which the more skilful (or more hazardous) architects of to-day suspend on a quarter of the same thickness. For an American building, it had some dignity of age. It was its steeple or tower which is memorable as the high place to which Dr. Franklin ascended when occupied with some electric experiments, on which his restless mind was engaged, while he was on his way to Albany to attend the memorable Union convention of 1754. It had been a chosen and favorite house of worship for the old people of New York ; and when it died the decent death of being found territorially too valuable to be kept for the ancient associations and likings of a few people, the Rev. Dr. DeWitt uttered the parting words of blessing in the old language. It had quaint usages but a few years previous; for very strange it seemed to modern eyes to see " the clerk " place, in a series of blackboards on the wall, the number of the first psalm that was to be sung, as if for the benefit of those who came late. There was a fitness in this choice of a place for the utterance of Mr. Adams' oration ; for the scene which that oration celebrated was all acted in real life but a brief distance from the doors of the old church. So hall and orator were worthy of each other ; and it was, in all its accompaniments, one of the great historical events of our annals.

When I next saw Mr. Adams, it was at the breakfast-table in the Astor House. A number of years had passed; but I recognized " the rare and picturesque old man," as Mc Dowell, of Virginia, so beautifully designated him, when pronouncing one of the Congressional eulogies. He seemed in good spirits, and immediately entered into conversation with a gentleman near him, whom I judged, by his words and look, to be a packet-ship captain, — of a class of gentlemen who knew everybody, and were so often, for a voyage, at least, master of all around them, that their acquaintance included everywhere the wisest and worthiest.

To my delight, their conversation took the
agreeable direction of a talk about swimming;
perhaps led thither by the aquatic association of
the captain.   Mr. Adams took the lead at once,
and seemed quite pleased in alluding to his own
skill and experience as a swimmer; and he gave
the statement of his beginning, in words somewhat
memorable :   " I," said he, " learned to swim at
eleven years of age, in Boston harbor, alongside
the frigate Alliance, *in thirty feet water.*"

It was type of his varied and momentous career,
— so often struggling alone in the conflicting tides
of public opinion, — that he learned to swim in
deep water.   The Alliance, it will be remembered,
was one of the vessels of war that were under
command of our great naval hero of the Revolution, John Paul Jones, of whom Walter Scott
says, that he frightened Edinburgh out of its wits,
and set " mine own romantic town " to all the
wisdom of its bailies to discover how they should
prevent his landing at Leith.   This must have been
just as Mr. Adams was going out with his father to
the latter's high diplomatic service.   Mr. Adams
then went on to tell his friend of his swimming
practice in the Potomac, every day, when he was
President of the United States.   He said this with
a particularity, which, in a lesser man, would have
seemed a little like calling this dignified fact into

recollection. I was very much obliged to the mariner for his presence, in thus leading Mr. Adams to talk about himself.

Governor Bradish dilated to me on the extraordinary versatility of Mr. Adams' acquirements, illustrating it by reference to his having seen him finish an entertainment of a dinner party by standing on the table and reciting a French play. But Charles King declared that one thing Mr. Adams could not do, — that was, write poetry ; and that he had, before this, been forced to express this opinion to him editorially, especially in relation to the poem of Dermot McMarrough. It is quite likely that he could not do what is so seldom an ability mingled with the qualities of a statesman. His life was a poetic one, for it touched the varieties of human experience, except that he never seemed to have known what it was to feel pecuniary want. He was defeated and almost proscribed, and rose above it with an increasing fame. He saw about all that was best in both the Old and New World, knew the wisest and greatest of all countries in civilization, and died in his duty.

It is a fact, not generally known, that he visited Washington just before going forth on his diplomatic career, being advised to do so. It would have been a picture worth perpetuation, this meeting of the keen, quick, resolute young man, in all his consciousness of the value of history, with the grand old man, who, with himself, had such strong ideas of what a republic should show itself in the eyes of the world. Mr. Adams had very little idea of the arts of popularity, though, 1 doubt not, he fully liked the thing itself. "How can he expect to be reëlected," said one of his friends, "when he gives you his hand to shake as stiff as a shingle?"

That was a memorable speech and occasion of one, which was heard and witnessed by the citizens of Albany, when Mr. Adams addressed an impromptu crowd from the "stoop" (I must use the Albany word) of Matthew Gregory's house, in the row now absorbed by Congress Hall. He had felt that the people of New York moved with him on his journey, and he knew the words which were the key-note of their heart. That speech was admirably reported by Sherman Croswell, who was a master of his art. Mr. Adams defied and outlived calumny, and did that wonderful thing, — he made a lesser station the occasion of fame and reputation to him after he had occupied the greater. He almost, more than any other of our great men, could not rest and did not rest. Learning to swim in deep water, he never sought the safety of the shallower.

While he was President, there was a party given at the White House, which derived most of its celebrity from some clever stanzas, written on its occasion, in which the brilliant or distinguished people who were likely to be there were mentioned, and whose refrain was long remembered:

> "Beaux and belles and maids and madams,   .
> All are gone to Mrs. Adams'."

I think there was a quiet but strong feeling in this country very much gratified, when Charles Francis Adams, his son, received the place of Minister to England, as it was a genealogy of diplomatic service which looked like stability. It helped us to combat the idea, that, in our country, there is no procession of talent.

There are few things in our history as remarkable as the prediction made by Mr. Adams, of the consequences which would follow the annexation of Texas. In years hence, when the calm and just historian (whose name, at this moment, happens to be unknown) shall write our record, the extraordinary document, in which the future was so portrayed, will be studied by every one.

He did not write poetry, — Mr. King was right; but he sometimes did succeed in verse; and the most felicitous of all his stanzas are those in which he gives a catalogue of his wishes; and it is momentous in their review, that he seems to have been favored in a degree, and not a minute degree, with the realization of all, — wealth, honors, station, fame, the pleasant, and even the luxurious, things of life. While he had to wait for some of these, at length they came; and he had, as nearly as it could be said of any of our public men, enjoyed, in the end, the harmony of a completed career; and those publications which his son is editing will be another wonderful chapter in that history.

He was deprived of a reëlection to the presidency for causes and with consequences, which, as this is not a political history, it is not for these pages to relate. I do not doubt, that, all his life, he felt it to be a deep personal wrong; for he was conscious of having served his country faithfully, and he had seen, just before him, Mr. Monroe's eight accorded years of quiet and easy success, and he knew, that, while Mr. Monroe was a very excellent man, himself had been one of the main arches of his administration.

General Jackson was the new and triumphant arrival into the presidency. With opinions about that remarkable man which may be prejudices, but which, I believe, had a foundation which the calmer reflection of maturer years approves, I concede that, in the only interview I ever had with him, the impression was a pleasant one; for, although he looked sufficiently stern and, perhaps, severe, yet he had a courtesy of manner, when he chose to exercise it, which was potential; and I have heard this stated, also, by the Rev. Dr. Campbell, of Albany, who knew all about him, who did not like him, and who maintained against him successfully a question in his department of action. I can see the old General even yet, in his room at the White House, talking so pleasantly with me about the only topic on which I happened to know anything that interested him, — the health of his friend, the Old Patroon of Albany. When I say, a pleasant manner, I mean gravely pleasant, and, of course, in dignity. Mr. Van Kleeck, of Albany, who might be said to know all mankind, was my guide to the grandeur of the White House.

. Dr. Campbell's account of him illustrated the fact that he had two lives going on at the same moment, — that of the quiet, remote man of his Tennessee existence, who liked the small horizon of his plantation and its in and out door incidents best, and his own life, as possessed of a great power, in which he bore no contradiction, and in which he would express opinions which it was quite clear were rather of limited than enlarged view of public affairs. But he had the confidence of the people in a degree that few others have possessed, and the way is not clear for his annals in their full truth yet. They will be written when we shall be possessed with the great and good idea that the truth is, after all, the very essence of valuable history.

I recollect being at Boston when the news of General Jackson's death arrived there. It seemed to me to awaken very little notice. I think the administration of the General, however important at the time, was, in its effects, much sooner effaced than it was, in his day, supposed possible; and the reason is, that it was a personal administration; and after General Harrison was subsequently, as a successful soldier, elected, that incident in our history was not alone.

When the General was at New York, a vast crowd was gathered before the City Hall. He looked out at it, and, turning to Mr. Hubbell, said, " There are no nullifiers there."

General Harrison finishes the list of the presidents who were born before our country ceased to be a colony of Great Britain. His frontier life had made him, comparatively, a stranger on the seaboard, and he came, in 1836, before the people rather by his history than by any personal associations. His death, after the one month of presidential power, startled the whole country, as, first of all our chief rulers, he died while in possession of the first place. I was told that during the month he lived in the White House, his hospitality and his plans for hospitality were unbounded; that he construed the welcome of the mansion almost up to its chanted promises, and that nothing could have averted severe financial embarrassment.

I asked Mr. Clay about the General. " Ah ! " said he, " he was a good-hearted, clever old gentleman.   When he was preparing for his inauguration, he sent to me his address, and suggested to me to erase anything in it that I did not approve ; and, with this permission, I *did* run my pencil through some passages.   Soon afterward he met me, and said, ' Mr. Clay, I have adopted all your suggestions except in those paragraphs that mention the Greeks and Romans.   Why, Mr. Clay,' said General H., ' when I was in Congress, somebody was searching for me, and looking into the hall of representatives, could not see me, but he heard somebody making a speech, and saying something about the Greeks and Romans. " That's him ; that's Harrison ! " said he.   Mr. Clay you must leave me those.' "

This incident, thus related by such distinguished authority, proves that General Harrison had great good humor and great good sense.

There was something grand in the fact that General Harrison had stood up, in Congress, the sole representative of all the great north-west, — a grandeur that we, and those who shall come after us, shall best know as we see to what that north-west has arisen. He was to its civilization what Daniel Boone had been to its barbarism, the representation of that which was to come,— the new life, in which the dominion of the intellectual over the material was to be developed.

General Harrison's father-in-law, John Cleves Symmes, was of the pioneer stock; but he was lifted up into the world's observation chiefly by the theory which he promulgated, that this was a hollow world (and, in one sense, we all believed and yet believe him), enterable at the poles, and that strange and momentous discoveries awaited those who should find way thither, and that, in some way, the northern lights issued thence. On this theme I heard him lecture at the Uranian Hall, Albany, and remember that, when he read his manuscript, he was prosy and dull, and that when he went off into extempore episodes, he was bright and interesting. His ideas had plausible place in their day of utterance, and encountered what has been the fate of all projectors, the semi-ridicule, semi-illustration of a book called Symzonia, in which the visit inter-spherical was, with vivid adventures, accomplished. His theory at last melted away like the stories of the Arcadia or the southern continent.

General Harrison's name, in its political sobriquet of "Tippecanoe," exercised the vocal powers of more men than this country has ever before or since found with will or capacity for song. As, in this volume, political history is only incidentally introduced, this theme of the great song of 1840 may but be glanced at. Its refrain was heard in all varieties of human intercourse, and a stranger then for the first time coming among us would have believed that the reputation of Germany, for popular singing — I may not say melody — had found formidable rivalry.

How many side-lights were thrown amidst the scholars of the old days of our French war and Revolution, by the conversation of the old men and the old soldiers, who, rising to no special rank or place, told us of the curious people that they had known, or the curious scenes in which they had intermingled. I use the word French war to designate the period in which our ancestors thought that their very existence was bound up in maintaining the supremacy of England's power over that of the Bourbons; and, as the great questions of government and of right really were in that day, their action was correct. It is a singular incident that General Washington did not designate the war in which we achieved independence, by the term in which it was always named, — the Revolution, — but as, " our dispute with Great Britain."

Even as late as 1810, a meeting was called of " all officers and soldiers who served one or more campaigns in the old French war," " to petition Congress for the recovery of our rights." Alas for the chance of the rights that had waited from 1754 till 1810! This meeting was probably got up by a Henry Watkins, who served in the French war, was present at the siege of the Moro Castle, and escaped being blown up by being absent on an errand, served in the revolutionary war, and made a show of going out in the war of 1812. A campaigner of such varied experiences might be excused for holding on to his right of recovery.

It must be recollected that our ancestors made up their record of life in a country where they had all the eventful variety of circumstance that could come to them, placed midway between their necessary entanglement with the dissensions of Europe, — very far off quarrels, imperfectly understood, and not the less eagerly championed, — and the barbarism which in the guise of the yet somewhat powerful Indian tribes gave them continual annoyance and trouble. The open, square, broad warfare of all that civilization can present, warring against itself, they did not know. To them the forest was the representative of a treacherous friend and vindic-

8

tive enemy; and the sea was the messenger of
alarm as often as the old dynasties of Europe ministered to their ambition by war.

A letter is before me from a Major-General in
the revolutionary army, dated 1780, which shows
how, as face answereth unto face in a mirror, do
the features of a great war find resemblance. In
this letter we can see the mastery of gold over all
transactions at all times. The perplexed General
is writing to an officer in the department of the
Commissary-General, and he says: "The unexpected disappointments met with from every quarter from which I expected supplies are likely to be
attended with the worst consequences, and call
upon us to repeat and redouble our exertions.
The occasion of all these disappointments is said
by all to be the want of money in the purchasing
departments, which the purchasers say has not
only put it out of their power to make sufficient
contracts, but has also prevented their sending up
the small stock of supplies they have been able to
preserve. I am therefore compelled, in order to
relieve the pressing necessities of the army, to fall
upon a measure extraordinary perhaps in its nature,
but rendered by that necessity unavoidable. We
will therefore endeavor to contract for the supplies
necessary for the support of this department upon
the following terms. You will purchase the sup-

plies at the cheapest price possible for *hard* money
to be paid October 1 ; and if it cannot be paid in
coin at that time, you may engage that those of
whom you purchase shall be paid in paper money
in the proportion it bears to gold and silver at
the time of payment, so that there shall be no loss
by depreciation ; and you may assure them that
rather than that there should be any failure the
public property should be sold."

And thus we find our fathers, in the dark and
"hard winter" time of 1780, reading the same
page of finance that later years have read to their
descendants.

I met an old soldier, by the name of Parks, who,
in 1847, stated himself as one hundred and five
years old; but that was not so. He was only
ninety-seven, if I may use the word *only* of longevity like that. He told us of his perilous adventures in the Sullivan campaign, — a wild series of
adventures, in regard to which the stories are free
to ally themselves with white man or Indian, according to the information or imagination of the
narrator. The old man illustrated the want of
material for long marching, which embarrassed the
armies of those days, by his recital of his being
compelled to wade across one of the lakes. He
told me of his memory of the effect of the earth-
quake of 1755, — that great trembling of the earth

in which the dread catastrophe of Lisbon occurred ; of the shaking of the little diamond panes of glass in the windows, — and this was doubtless true, for so much of it was experienced in North America.

Major Adam Hoops, a choice relic of the revolutionary officer, prompt, erect and decided, had been an aid of Sullivan, and lived to see the harvests of the white man smile, where he and those with him had devastated all that the Indian had cultured. He had a very different idea of Brandt's history from that given by Mr. Stone's Life of the famed Thayandenagea.

How strangely in the loom of life the hands of war and peace — red as is one and white as is the other — grasp together in Progress. An old batteau or flat-boat used by that invading army in the tortuous and perilous voyage down the Susquehanna, was, as it was left to decay, taken to the Seneca and then to Cayuga, by those who went thither to make the " settlement."

In their trip on the Seneca, they passed over a route which another journey has made more famous.

He who kept the French throne warm for the completion of the time when " the empire " should be ready for " the nephew of his uncle," was once, like that nephew, a wanderer in our own land, taking a larger circle of travel, however, than the

more concentrated, silent man, who waitèd and
waited, and won at last. * Louis Philippe had been
at Canandaigua, the guest of Thomas Morris, — a
man himself always memorable, and whose very
lovely wife — of the beautiful Kane family — I
saw, as a widow, in 1843, at Boston ; and, as illustrating the rise of the country, this lovely lady
told me that her bridal journey was on horseback
to Canandaigua. Thomas Morris was, in after
life, a favorite guest of John Jacob Astor, and his
conversation did much to enliven that table.

Mr. Morris gave letters to a citizen of Elmira,
which was called at that time, by a great poverty
of variety in nomenclature, Newtown. George
Mills, of the Chemung low country, who was living in 1848, remembered the royal Frenchman.
He had come from Geneva, down the Seneca lake,
in a schooner, just built by the Captain William-
son who, at one time, had thought of buying all
the country which is now Ohio. Louis Philippe
took the journey from the head of Seneca lake to
Elmira ; and it was good taste to do so, for a love-
lier land seldom the sun elsewhere looks upon.
At Elmira, the travellers took a boat down the
Susquehanna, stopping, I suppose, to refresh himself with his own language at Frenchtown.

A few years since, Mr. Brodhead, the accomplished historian, procured for me a map of the

king's route, approved by the king himself, which
I gave to one of the steamboat proprietors of the
Seneca lake. Time gives value to these authentic
illustrations of history, when the record of the life
of the rulers of men becomes all that is preserved
of the annals of the ages.

One by one I have seen — and seen with sorrow — our people demolish the physical structures
that were evidences in the stories of the past. To
the miserable narrowness or indifference of public
sentiment that permitted John Hancock's house to
be sacrificed, I have already alluded; and that is
but one of many. The grounds of old battle-
fields, which might have been preserved as public
property, have been unnecessarily levelled. In
that wonderful city, Chicago, the block-house was
the type of its youth. It told, better than statistics, what sudden life had come to that lap of the
lakes, and yet, down it went! So did Fort Stanwix; and it is questionable if our eyes would yet
be rejoicing in the picturesque ruins of Ticonder-
oga, but that the golden step of fashion-travel led
that way, and what, in other places, had been denied to history, was there preserved to gain.

The Declaration of Independence was first read
to the citizens of Albany by Matthew Visscher,
standing in front of the then City Hall, at the
north-east corner of Court (South Broadway) and

Hudson street. The gathering was tumultuous, because there was a popular belief that the reading was to be prevented by the inroad of those who, as yet, adhered to the old government.

Now such a scene as that was, deserves, in the annals of an ancient city, some local remembrance ; for this aid to memory is old as the stones set up for the swellings of Jordan. As our country grows old, very old, all these incidents will be sought for, and sometimes with utterly false results. I have made one of a formal and elaborate procession to the Rock of Plymouth, when all that I could see or find of it was a small remainder, more than half hid in the debris of a commercial wharf, and another piece broken off and carried " up street."

The field of Runnymede, which clarifies so many perorations in speeches about wresting our liberty and our rights out of the hands of tyrants, is even yet, so some one recently told me, a tilled field ; and that the Old World has set all such associations in the crystal of song and story is, at this hour, the occasion of the journey thither of thousands. Our metropolis has neglected its treasure of historical association. They have passed away, one by one ; and now, all that we can do is to admire the good work by which the Historical Society, like Old Mortality, regraves the words on crumbling stone, too often amidst the mist of doubt, that neglect alone has raised.

The voice of the wise man tells us not to say that the former days were better than these ; and I obey the counsel, as well I may.   The age of progress and prosperity in which we live is indeed far better for all the material, and, perhaps, for all the mental, interest of man.   Far more smoothly and sweetly, in our day of peace, the stream of our life moves on ; but so much the more do we enjoy the contrast of the tumultuous and bold scenes, in which the ancient colonies, with all their romance of loyalty to crowns and dynasties, to old families and to ancestral names, became new and powerful states, known in their own .name and own right to the earth.   We feel all this the keener, as in the stormy day of the winter the luxury of the home-hearth is brightest.

I have detained my reader, over repeated apologies, for so long, by the side of these days, reluctant to leave them.   They are pictures not again to be painted, — dramas not again to be acted.   When again shall any man arise among us, in whom it would be in the recognized fitness of things that we should see him, as Washington was seen when he delivered his inaugural address, " dressed in a full suit of the richest black velvet, with diamond knee-buckles and square, silver buckles set upon shoes japanned with the most scrupulous neatness, black silk stockings, his shirt ruffled at breast and wrists, a light dress sword, his hair powdered," and thus uttering to Congress and the people the words of a purity and a patriotism, *in whose truth they all believed.*

Do we often think how, in the strange things of history, it was, that Washington died just at the close — the closing days, of the old century, as if time had no work for him in that new and wonderful volume which it opened on the first day of January, 1800 ? The pilot left the helm just as the stormy election of that year was to agitate the sea of affairs, and he was spared the delicate difficulties which surrounded a man who had united all hearts.

A few years passed away, and the slow dignity of the old ways saw its decadence in the success of Mr. Fulton's efforts to make steam the servant of the wants of man. I heard the recollections of two very interesting companions, in different spheres of action, of Mr. Fulton. Judge Wilson, of Albany, was of those who accompanied him in the first of all his Hudson River voyages. A Quaker friend remonstrated with Mr. Wilson on trusting himself with " such a wild fowl " as this most absurd structure was believed to be by all practical people. But those who had essayed to follow Fulton in this bold movement were not to be kept off by ridicule ; and to his imperfect and rude boat they went, and off *it* went, and it stopped, and the crowd on the wharf jeered, and Fulton felt as if the laugh touched his inmost heart by its sarcasm; but he believed in the might of the bubbling steam, and his boat went on, and — the new chapter in the world's history was plainly to be read on the Hudson River.

In 1851, that extraordinary " excursion " was made, in which the liberality of the Chicago and Rock Island Railroad Company displayed to a thousand guests the grandeur, and not less, the beauty, of the Upper Mississippi. Such hospitality was beyond the old stories of the princely entertainments of Blenheim and Chatworth.

Of all that we saw, we saw most and best the river, the Mississippi. I recollect that we gave cheers as we came in sight of it. The river, the river, its exquisite, park-like scenery, those bluffs, in beauty beyond our dreamings, so calm and majestic, so varied in every mile of its magnificent progress, — it has neither parallel nor rival. And this proud river we had ascended quietly and resistlessly, overcoming its rapids, conquering its currents, pressing on, as though our course was over a smooth lake; and we owed this to the genius of Robert Fulton. And this great triumph was witnessed by one who had been his chosen, his intimate friend, — Mr. Waldo, a name known to all familiar with the history of American painters. A very pleasant old artist he was, of cultivation and taste and kindly manner, bright faculties, and active mind. He had been the companion and fellow-scholar of Fulton. While together, they pursued the study of painting under the tuition of Benjamin West, the president of the Royal Academy. While engaged in the task of the painter, the mind of Fulton was occupied with the steam-engine. It was building in mental fabric, shaft, valve, cylinder, in his brain, and he looked forward to a nobler success. He told Mr. Waldo that the great triumph for him would be the use of the steamboat on the Mississippi. There, he said, was to be the scene of his victory.

And yet Fulton thought that he was greatest in the fact that he had, as he thought, invented a sure instrument of destruction of hostile ships, by his submarine torpedo. So strangely inaccurate are men in determining even their own fame.

Chancellor Livingston, who was the friend and fellow-owner of the Fulton grant, it is said, after the introduction of other boats than their own, would not go to New York except by coach or carriage. It was a monstrous wrong in this State, that it did not stand by Fulton's exclusive right when it was attacked in processes of law. It is but a synonym of the word just, that the word "exclusive" was used. What inventor ever deserved reward, if this man did not? And although there may be ever so many finicalities of reasoning, — that somebody, prior to him, knew that steam had power, — it was his heart that dared, and his hand that ventured, the application of the power to great practical use. Steamboats, that could move against wind and tide, — those were the things accomplished by Fulton. I heard a brief word of the argument in the Court of Errors, when Thomas Addis Emmet was heard for the heirs of Fulton. It was in this argument, that he interwove with his reasoning a pleasantry; for I suppose the characteristic fancy of his country did not desert him in his exile. "They tell you," said he, "that this is a coasting question" (the assertion on the other side was that New York had no power to grant a privilege affecting a coasting voyage); "but I say, that you might rather call it, as far as our own Hudson river is concerned, a *banking* question."

The heirs of Robert Fulton, since his life was too brief for the enjoyment of the reward himself, ought to have been as opulent as the nation could have made its greatest benefactor. I remember to have been a witness, in 1828, or thereabout, to a grant by Morgan Lewis, acting for the representatives of so much of the franchise as was yet left to

them, of the right, till 1836, to navigate one of
the interior lakes of New York, where the tide did
not give " national " jurisdiction.

The history of the progress of steam-navigation
in this country, from Fitch's rude paddle-boat to
the grandeur of the St. John, would be, of itself,
a pleasant and valuable volume : but that is not in
the plan of this book. Yet it is illustrative of the
taste of the leading men of the period, or illustrative of the general education and influences, to notice what were the names or designation of the
very earliest boats. In official advertisements, as
late as 1808 and 1809 (the navigation beginning
in 1807), the owners designate their vessel yet as
the steamboat. First of all, came courtesies to the
distinguished Livingston, who had associated himself with the inventor, and Clermont, his manor-
house, and the Chancellor, his erminial title; and,
after that, something of an ornate fancy, — the
Paragon and the Car of Neptune, — flights of the
imagination which must have bewildered the plain
people of that day ; and then, the indication of
the widely-diffused feeling in respect to a then
recent, terrible calamity, the destruction by fire
of the Theatre at Richmond, in a boat bearing
that city's name.

Some old Indian's strange name, — Walk-in-
the-water, heralded the steam voyages on Lake

Erie, with that of the great man of the west, — Henry Clay ; and all American use of steam as a power on the ocean was led by a vessel bearing the name of one of the southern cities, — Savannah.

In these names, we can read rather of the local, than wide-spread or national, attention to the enterprise, at the time of its inception. In 1784, General Washington expressed himself as having been, to that time, a disbeliever in the ability of steam-power to overcome wind and current or tide ; but he concedes that Mr. Rumsey's power, then shown to him, has induced him to think that it may be done. He did not dream that every sea, lake, and river would possess steamboats bearing, as their proudest designation, his own name.

De Witt Clinton's admirable personal appearance is strongly impressed on my memory. Indeed, it remains as a page of singular dignity and courtliness in life's recollections, seeing the manner in which he bowed to some ladies whom he met in State street, — the hat completely off, and the homage such as, from Clinton, any lady might have given charming acknowledgment. Prefacing a notice of Governor Clinton by allusion to his courtesy might not be truthful indication of his general characteristics ; but of this I could only give the testimony of two very differing witnesses, both his abiding personal friends, and intimate with and thoroughly appreciative of him. Indeed, it was interesting to me to see how really great men such as, beyond all contradiction, were John C. Spencer and Dr. T. Romeyn Beck, could have taken such opposite views of one man.

Dr. Beck said, Clinton delighted to say cutting things to people around him, — things that hurt them; but Mr. Spencer said he thought the doctor in error, that Clinton was not a rude or sarcastic man, but that he had a great fondness for joking men, or, as the phrase is, for running them; and this was misconstrued as being sarcastic. Dr. Beck thought Clinton joked very hard, if it was all joke, and he doubted if Mr. Spencer was as likely as himself to know Clinton in familiarity.

I think it was the opinion of the time that Governor Clinton did not possess what is characterized as popular manners; but, in the face of all this, none of the great men of our State were ever so personally popular. Even the charming manners of Governor Tompkins, whose way of talking to men and talking with them, sent them from him delighted, even if all this pleasantness had contained a negative to their requests, even he could not concentrate to himself and on himself the favor of the people. It was thought that Clinton did not always receive kindly or rather welcome kindly the very efforts to aid him in his wishes or his affairs; but he had friends the most earnest and devoted, and was sustained in all circumstances and above all circumstances. This is the end of popularity, if it is not its way.

His party might and did go to wreck around him; but he stood up and triumphant amidst that wreck. The truth is, he was believed by the people to be, as he indeed was, a very great man; and the people felt that pride in their possession of such a man that they did not ask of him the perpetual step forward that seems necessary to the preservation of lesser men. Wherever the man of power, the man of government was to indicate himself, in all personal public position, there Governor Clinton was superb. I saw him in the midst of that which to him was of the greatest of triumphs, for it was the success of his own predictions of success, long adhered to, long maintained, against all forms of sarcasm and ridicule and obloquy. It was when he stood on the deck of the canal boat, — either the Seneca Chief or the Young Lion of the West, — and entered the Hudson River in the great opening day of the canals. There, surrounded by a group of the gentlemen of the chief cities of the seaboard and the towns of Western New York, he was the man to whom all looked; and although the highway bore the offi-

cial designation of the Erie Canal, it was the popular judgment, and they were right, that it should
be known as the Clinton Canal.   To him that day
was the proof that he was right as well as bold,
when he had pledged his political existence in the
fact that a route of internal. navigation from the
lakes to tide-water could be accomplished, and
that it was a revolution in the progress of the State
of New York and of the great domain then just
opening, which was known in the vague grandeur
of word as the West.   The. people exulted in looking at him ; and the great pageant of that era had
as its grandest feature the presence of De Witt
Clinton.   It *was* a lordly time throughout.   The
progress was a scene of earnest rejoicing, for it
told to all that the prosperity of the country received new impulses from those hours.

Arches were built, and all that the imperfect
condition of decorative art could suggest was
adopted to indicate the public festivity.   Greatest
of all was the aquatic procession, the flotilla of
steamboats in which Clinton proceeded in his journey to the ocean.   We were to know the very
moment of the mingling of the waters of the Erie
with the Atlantic by a common telegraph ; for
Mr. Morse in those days was thinking most of the
tints he was placing on canvas, and this new
voice of electricity, which to-day is talking all the

9

wide world around, had not been evoked by science. The cannon were placed so near to each
other that from Sandy Hook to Buffalo, sound
should blend with sound, and, quick as it could
travel, Buffalo should know that the waters were
one. I listened in earnest expectation to hear
the southern report which should be the signal for
the Albany gun on the pier to communicate the
news to north and west; but I believe I did not
hear it. Nevertheless, the gunner having his time-
table and knowing when he ought to have heard
by that, believed, as in Prussia, that all things are
regulated, and let his cannon speak. To-day San
Francisco might hear before the vase was dry from
which the water was poured.

And yet attached to and identified with the
great canal system as was Governor Clinton, he
saw clearly what was to be the use and preëmi-
nence of railways. There was a small model of a
railway in the executive room at Albany, and he
led one of the members of Assembly from a western
county to it, and said to him, " Here, sir, is the
way in which you are yet to reach this city."

To appreciate fully what was Clinton's exultation
at being the master figure in the scene of the
canal's triumph in completion, we must have stood
with him in that day at Rome, so many years previous, when he saw and participated in the re-

moval of the first earth for the work, — a shovel-
ful of dirt taken from a field near the decaying ramparts of old Fort Stanwix. There was a grandeur of
self-reliance in believing that to be the new token
of a completed river over all the very long distance
that separated Lake Erie and the Hudson River.

I saw him when his appearance, from the peculiar condition of the public mind, elicited great
attention. It was when he, in company with the
Patroon, headed a procession of the order of free-
masons, garnished and glittering in the regalia of
the brethren.

I recollect that I was employed by a friend of
his to make a copy of his last message to the Legislature of New York, and that the introductory
words, as he wrote them, were, " Fellow-citizens
of the Senate and House of Representatives," as
if he had, at the moment, been thinking of Congress, and then he had erased " of Representatives," and substituted the proper form of " Assembly." He was so kind as to approve the manner in which the copy was made ; and I remember,
in his note so stating, he used a word which was
then unusual, and which then seemed to me quite
in the dignities, — " the chirography is good."

No one who was in Albany at the time can
forget the evening of his death, or the occasion and
day of his funeral. I was sitting in a public read-

ing-room at the time,— the evening of the 11th of
February, 1828,— and a gentleman entered, hur-
riedly saying, " *He* is dead ! " We did not need
explanation or further comment to know to whom
this referred. We felt it must be Clinton ; and as
the tidings of his sudden departure spread, the
feeling was absorbing.   I have never, on any
other occasion of public loss, witnessed any such
deep, earnest, pervading grief as was felt in relation to his death.   It was the sudden going out of
a great light,— the sharply quick closing of a great
career, in which all were interested ; for it seemed
to be a universal opinion that the tide was rising
which was, beyond all doubt, to bear him to the
presidency ; as, indeed, much of the friendly feeling to General Jackson covered, as its strongest
element, the belief that Governor Clinton was to
be at his side and his successor.

His remains were laid out in state, as I think it
may not improperly be designated in this instance,
and there was a great concourse of people, who
moved around the coffin, gazing at his face.   I
recollect being impressed with the simplicity of the
inscription on the coffin-plate :

" De Witt Clinton,
Died
February 11, 1828,
While Governor of the State of New York."

The scene of the public funeral, which, in something of grandeur, was conducted by the authority of the Legislature, was very remarkable in its sincerity of sorrow. A great multitude gathered around the house, which was that known as the Banyer House, on the south-east corner of Steuben and North Pearl streets, and the long procession made its way to a private vault,— a little stone building in one of the upper western streets.

The suddenness of this death was a shock to the public feeling. It put an end at once to a large chapter of political purpose, and it seemed to begin at once the era of new measures, and to admit into broader and stronger light those to whom Clinton had been the one obstacle that could not be removed.

And yet this ought not to have been an occurrence unexpected. The clear and prophetic skill of the eminent David Hosack had declared, months previous, that Governor Clinton could not live beyond the then coming March, and his judgment was only too true. I think that at this day, as then, the status of Governor Clinton, as a great man, is of the very first of all New York's list. It may be to this hour a theme of regret, that the first place in the government of the nation was not filled by him. In a better sense than Keats used it of himself, it may be said of Clinton — the canal being his memorial — "his name is writ in water."

Governor Clinton was run to the eyelashes — as the sporting men say — in his last contest, when William B. Rochester was selected to run against him. I know that there was the greatest anxiety manifested by Governor Clinton's warmest friends in relation to his success, and the figures looked very ugly for a long time; and he who was so suddenly powerful, was washed ashore on the beach of the Atlantic, after a wild and fierce storm, which wrecked the steamship in which he was a passenger; and "Mr. Rochester, a cabin passenger," was all the record that the chronicle of the hour made. The State of New York was spared the sorrow — I will not use any other word, lest it might seem as of political reflection — of the thought that defeat had met De Witt Clinton. He took the name which had been eminent and powerful even in our colonial days, and with which the history of the State had commenced, and made it the pride of the State. No wonder was it that the State, forgetting all party feeling, should have made for him a deep and sincere mourning. And yet the State did not do for his great service what would have been done in England for a statesman whose policy had so practically benefitted it; and through whom it had be-

come the great highway of all the north, fearing
the subtle and hidden injury,—very subtle and
hidden, which is said to exist in the remembrance,
after their terms of service have closed, — New
York coldly turned aside, and gave the name of
Clinton a place, as Mr. Jefferson says, " among
the worthies who deserve from mankind an ever-
lasting remembrance " — but that was all.

We have avoided a pension list for civil service,
and Clinton's great work for his State remained
unrewarded.   Fulton was thrust out of his franchise ; Jefferson strained his ingenuity and his
morality to devise a lottery in his old age, as a
means of getting money to make his extreme old
age comfortable.   It is not too late for us yet to do
what will cost us nothing, — to give to the canal
the designation of the Clinton canal.   It is no
more in its results of Erie than of Michigan or
Huron.   The most remote corner of Lake Michigan furnishes more tonnage to the canal than do
all the shores of lake Erie.   Is this suggestion but
an imaginative one?   It may be so, yet it may
find its palliation in admiration for this great
statesman of New York.

Of Governor Tompkins, that pleasant and popular man of the people, I recollect only seeing his
entry into Albany with something of a public reception.   General Wickham, of Goshen, related

to me an incident which the Governor told of himself, while enjoying the hospitalities (and cordial and generous they were) of Mr. Wickham's house. He said that he found himself a judge of the Supreme Court at a very early age; for the zeal of his party to do him honor was not to be restrained by the bounds of a cold prudence. It was a formidable thing to be a judge in that day.

. Well, one of the first circuits to be held by the young judge was that of Scoharie county, and one of the first questions to be decided was whether a certain old deed, produced in evidence, was an ancient instrument which proved itself; and the argument, by the grave and venerable and learned counsellors, the Van Vechtens and Henrys and Cadys, was astute and profound, quite enough to bewilder the judge, who, in despair, looked at the deed, and, as he said, saw by its worn and musty appearance that it was of any supposable age; and so he decided, and was thus relieved of the argument which he felt was only bewildering him.

He presided at the Constitutional Convention of 1821, where the good and great and wise of our State met to give a new constitution,— one of the first surges of that great unrest and discontent with the tested and the proved, which the verse thus condenses :

" All things old are over old ;
Nothing new is new enough ;
We will teach mankind that *we* can make
A world of better stuff."

How much better the physical is in our early recollection than the intellectual, is illustrated by all of us. A great flood, a great fire, a vivid color, a comet, is remembered when association with the great and the gifted has left no impression on us. I once endeavored to find out the date of marriage of an elderly person who was unlettered. She could not state how long her married life had been, but when asked, " Were you married before or after *the* eclipse, the great eclipse ? " then she answered promptly enough, " The year after."

Of all that convention I recollect nothing of its session except seeing Governor Tompkins in the chair ; but I have a distinct impression of the sensation created throughout Albany by the sudden death of Mr. Jansen, one of the representatives of Ulster county, while attending the exhibition of Peale's great picture, " The Court of Death." The mournful coincidence was in all hearts and on all tongues.

Through what a succession of celebrated and illustrious names the ownership of the mansion, once occupied by Governor Tompkins, has passed, to end in the best of all uses — that of a church !

Yates, and Tompkins, and Seward, and the Kanes. It is not a local record alone that is written in these, and the annals of whatever is courteous and brilliant would, for the appreciation of all, be imperfectly written if these were excluded.

She is dead whose name is most imperishably associated with that house when it was the residence of Oliver Kane. In beauty, glittering; in wit, brilliant; in personal fascination, unequalled; in thought, expression, conversation, impressive, original, winning, — she made the hours passed with her, radiant; and it is of the most impressive of all monitions of the fading of all that is loved or lovely, to have seen her name in the catalogue of the grave.

That convention, over which Governor Tompkins presided, included names that might claim the best memories of the country. Did it enumerate in its list any greater man than Elisha Williams? It is not possible that the universal plaudit bestowed on his powers, by all who remember him, can be in error. He must have been great who could deserve all this. A sharp examination of a witness is all that I can personally recollect of him; but every man that heard him, talks rapturously about his charm of word. Especially did William Kent talk to me about him; and to have been praised by William Kent was high eulogy. The

choice word, the exquisite figure, the persuasive
manner, the denunciation, the sarcasm, if those
were the weapons he desired to use. I heard some
one say that it was ascertained afterwards that
much of that which seemed the brilliant creation
of the instant was the prepared and arranged work
of study; and yet, such is the conflict of testimony about all, men, I was also informed that he
did not write easily. It is possible to reconcile all
this. The fancies of men come fast and flashing.
To be preserved in that which can be available,
the process of writing, may be slow indeed ; as
used afterwards, the act of utterance may give to
them again all that was brilliant and glowing.
We can all understand this when we know that
Moore's rose-leaf words, which fall with such soft-
ness on the ear, were closely examined and tested
before they were marshalled into metrical arrangement; and that Campbell's grand lyrics were
thought about, and thought around, and all over,
and beat out. Whether by preparation or impulse, Williams rose in the court or in the legislature, the master of the hour, and courts, and juries,
and conventions obeyed the talisman. Perhaps he
was not as confident of success as Dudley Marvin,
another most remarkable man, who said of some
unfortunate prisoner, " He did not employ me,
and he was hung."

When Governor Tompkins and Governor De Witt Clinton held the station of chief magistrate of New York, they had great power of patronage. Under the constitution of 1777 and 1821, they were, to a great extent, the " fountains of honor." They managed this perilous power very differently. The one made himself the delight of the people; the other, it is true, sustained himself, but it was by the force of his talent against his deficiency in that excellent little virtue of mind — tact. Governor Clinton was over-careful, and brought worlds of trouble on himself. When an office was vacant, and a candidate presented himself, he said, " Let us wait, perhaps there will be others; " and of course others, by the quantity, presented themselves, and of the many only one was fortunate; the others went home to consider themselves greatly aggrieved men. Not so with Governor Tompkins. When the place was vacant, if the man that asked first was a worthy and proper recipient, he gave him the place at once. Others came for it; he heard them, said he had made a choice, would have been happy to have seen them first; why did they not come sooner? Each man went home convinced that it was not Governor Tompkins' fault that the office was not theirs. *He*, the Governor, was a noble and a true-hearted man. Their loss had been in their own negligence, and hence Daniel D. Tompkins was the delight of the people.   ·

I suppose that in the political annals of this State, the people were never in a greater embarrassment of good, than when called on to choose for their Governor — as they were in 1816 and 1820 — between Tompkins and Rufus King, Tompkins and De Witt Clinton. We can imagine the bewildered election and the perplexed suffrage, and that there was the contented feeling that the result, in either case, must be a great victory.

Ambrose Spencer, who took such strong and determined grasp of the business of that convention, as he did of all that came before him in life, was ever to me the personification of a ruler,— not of a judge,— distinguished as he is in the memories of men and in the record for eminence in the latter department of human action ; but it was difficult to imagine that man of almost resistless utterance of opinion, amounting, in the onset, to decision — to think of him as calmly balancing and adjusting all that could be said before him in relation to the merits or the appearances of a case. I would rather have thought of him as at once seeing the right, and that the argument, in all beyond the presentation of facts, must have been restraint on his impatience. He looked the character of a ruler, not bending to the impulses of the hour, but with the possession of constant power; and he, like his son, never understood the figure second, as applicable to himself. I do not, by any means, intend this as implying self-sufficiency or vanity, not at all, but self-reliance, — that way which seems to assert for itself unity, independence, almost isolation. His high nature revolted at the tyranny of others. Perhaps he would have exercised it himself. Of that I cannot judge accurately. He could not abide General Jackson; and it was as amusing as it was interesting to hear him, as I have done, at a public meeting, vehemently denounce the loss of self-control on the part of the President, and — lose his own.

I saw him meet Erastus Root on the steps of the Capitol, when, in 1839, the vicissitudes of politics had brought them within the fold of one party. General Root was standing, I thought, rather awkwardly and embarrassed, and as if not quite certain what to do when Judge Spencer should come up to him. The Judge very quickly relieved him, for he walked on as stern and unswerving and erect as if no truce of political exigency had united their long-severed political affinities.

In 1840, a large political delegation of young and active men went from Ithaca to Owego, to attend a political meeting at the latter place. We had a new locomotive, which was of the most impulsive character, and its fondness for a rest every mile or two was remarkable. The Judge was with us, and excessively disturbed by the hindrances to our journey; at all which I could not be impatient, for the engine was the effort of a most self-sacrificing enterprise to furnish additional ease to the traveller on that route. Of course there was nothing very extraordinary or improper in being greatly annoyed at a delayed journey; but it impressed me as not quite in the dignity of one who had seen so much of life's real vexations.

Yet, this must not be supposed to be in ignorance of the fact, that Judge Spencer was a man thoroughly possessed of the courtesies of life. I have too strong memory of personal kindness to doubt this for a moment.

In the National Convention of 1844, that nominated Henry Clay to the Presidency, Judge Spencer nominated Mr. Frelinghuysen for the Vice-Presidency. He did it, for he willed it; and his was that will which makes its own road through all obstacles. Mr. Frelinghuysen's nomination was a good one, but not a wise one. It is true, that whatever is good is wise; but it is equally wisdom, where a choice of good is presented, to take that which is also best for the hour. If political managers, who are often really great men, would more frequently study Sir Christopher Wren's epitaph, it would be to them the signal light of success.

When he died, solemn honors were given by the Legislature to a memory so worthy. The Governor and all the officers of State, the Senate and the Assembly, gathered at the obsequies, and one of the old Judiciary, Judge Woodworth, — who had been the witness of all the career of Spencer, — was present. The services were held in the old St. Peter's. I remember that the grouping of the scene at the funeral impressed me. There was James Kane, with his blue camlet cloak, the collar half up, his florid complexion, disarranged hair, listening — as that true-hearted gentleman always did — with the utmost attention; the five clergymen, coming in mournful step up the aisle, as the organ moaned forth its notes of dirge. I find that I made a memorandum, at the time, that the Legislature behaved like gentlemen. I hope this was not so unusual in the history of the times as to have been exceptional.

I have departed from my rule, in mentioning the name of Mr. Kane, for he was a private citizen; but his were those rare qualities of the unvarying gentleman; his association with the early mercantile history of the State had been so marked, — his companionship with, and knowledge

of, the leading men of the State so thorough,
that his name is not altogether out of place in a
retrospect of the times.

The roll of the really great men who were in
the Convention of 1821, is a long and historical
one. There, in that wonderful delegation of Co-
lumbia County, was Van Ness. Of him the testimony is, that in intellect he was gigantic; his
sway over the heart irresistible. I have heard
Mr. Joshua A. Spencer relate of his powers of
conversation, that, in attendance at a circuit, when
the lawyers were gathered at the ordinary tea-
table of the tavern, — which in and on itself had
nothing whatever to detain them at it, — such
was the fascination of his talk, that they all lingered around him until the night passed away,
and the morning sun surprised the intellectual
revellers. Van Ness belonged to a family who
took high mental rank, and in all the departments
of public action made their names remembered for
their talent.

Not that they were in the Convention, but that
amidst the roll of the eloquent men of that period,
they were eminent, I would like to have known
something of Baent Gardinier and of Henry R.
Storrs. The first has a traditional reputation of
brilliancy, and the latter is of the first names in
the legal annals of our State. I once asked Mr.

10

Thurlow Weed, whose opportunities of observation and accuracy in those opportunities were unequalled, who had impressed themselves upon his memory as the most eloquent men heard by him. He deliberated some time before he answered, and then said, " John Duer and Henry R. Storrs ; " and it must have been that Mr. Storrs deserved this high tribute of praise. I have a personal mournful association with his name. Some months before these pages were written, Mr. William Curtis Noyes, the graceful and distinguished counsellor, had arranged with me to join him in preparing a life of Mr. Storrs, especially in view of a journal or diary which Mr. Storrs had kept, and which was then to be in the care of Mr. Noyes. It has since been placed in the archives of the Buffalo Historical Society.

Gardinier and Storrs blended the life of the lawyer with the statesman, having very ably filled congressional place; and were both recognized as men to whom the impatient ear of Congress would give its rare attention.

We lost power in the North when we ceased to have such men in our representation. Mr. Clay remembered well the career of Mr. Storrs, and in a visit to Western New York alluded to it. There was a gathering of talent in and about the County of Oneida, which left its impress on the policy

and jurisprudence of the State for a long series
of years ; and the list of those who from that
home graced the capitol and the courts is a proud
page in her annals.   Before our volume is completed, we shall find another name that, though
brief in career, made even that brevity of life brilliant and powerful.

Mr. Storrs' great power as a debater made for
him a reputation any man would have envied, for
it is known that Mr. Clay said of him, — and that
without the prompting of any leading question, —
" that he was greatest in the House of Representatives of any man he had known.   He had great
power of reasoning, sufficiently rhetorical, but,
above all, forcible, — of commanding person, of fine
voice.   He saw far ahead, — he saw too far ; all
sides of a question presented themselves, and while
the mass by his side accepted and were swayed
by his reasoning, he left himself in doubt, and
went on and went into doubt, and from that, his
reasoning and his action dissevered."   At the close
of a speech, which brought the minds of men
right to him, it was not at all certain that his own
action would correspond to the word to which his
reasoning, irresistible to others, had led them.   He
seemed not to know how to grasp power, after
he had won it.   Hence Mr. Clay may be excused
for having added to his eulogy of Mr. Storrs, that,

with his greatness, he was also the most useless of all leading men.

And this has its parallel in a class of men who speak to themselves, who, from thought and study and philosophical analysis of their own judgment, overlook the fact that the kingdom within us, however all-important to ourselves, is, in truth, of very little interest to all exterior. An eminent debater in the State legislation of New York, Mr. Simmons, of Essex County, could reason well for hours; and it was easy for him to do so. He was talking to the Areopagi that sat on the Mars Hill of his own studies ; but the power to reach other men was not his. I name him, for he was eminent as an abstract reasoner. Mr. Storrs, it is true, did influence others, and that greatly ; but they were tired of following a man, who did not follow himself. All over the earth, — for it is of the weakness of human kind, — men will follow most closely a leader who, in some degree, commands their allegiance. The degree may not safely go to that which is arbitrary, but it will only be effectual if it is decisive. We find Mr. Storrs' name rather in the lesser biographies for this, when his talent was such as to deserve a foremost place, if he had but gone where his bright and glowing words went.

The controversies between the federal and

the democratic party occupied the thought and
words of these gifted men. Time holds an in-
verted telescope, and we see subjects of strife as
much smaller than they appeared to those who were
actors at the hour. Mr. Hammond, in his political history, gives the formal and didactic account
of these controversies, and the reason for them;
and although he was once so kind as to propose
that I should write the continuation of his history,
I am not to touch such themes, except as in illustration of more general history, in this volume.
In the far-off look at the debates and arguments
and addresses and resolutions and proceedings and
celebrations, we see that our quiet ancestors blazed
themselves into a great heat about the thesis of the
hour. They drove quiet from their days, — perhaps
very wisely, — that is, of the unsettled questions.
It is amusing to look at the far-off indignation.
The scowl of party violence almost darkened the
thresholds of Mount Vernon, and as to all other
households, it laid the very shadows of Egypt
across some of them. I have before me a notice
written by federals, of a celebration of the down-
fall of Napoleon I., which is so vituperative of the
democrats as to be ludicrous. It says: "The
democrats surrounded the tavern (Washington
Hall), with intent to commit the usual horrid dep-
redations concomitant with the nature of these

human monsters. The police had been prepared
in time, and when these savage orgies commenced
their infernal pranks, they were arrested on the
threshold of their pursuit, and were committed to
prison, among whom were some of their first char-
acters. The celebration of the day was held
with cheerful harmony and enthusiasm, with a
most able oration by the Hon. Governeur Morris."

Such was the temper of the times. We can, in
reading the above, better estimate the steady intellect of the great men who, amidst such storm of
opinions, were masters of all that was winning and
persuasive in human utterance.

CHAPTER IV.

UT we return to the Convention of 1821,—
for it was the full-dress party of the intellect
of that period,— each county having exerted
itself to send thither its wisest and worthiest.
So, too, did Virginia gather in that day its
noblest names to a similar Convention ; and
when James Madison rose to speak, such
was the crowd around him, that the reporter could
find place for his duty only at his feet.

I have alluded to the concentration of the intellect. of the State at the Convention of 1821.
This expression should be used in a more guarded
form. A close review of the lists of that Convention gives indeed a catalogue of many names, each
of whom was eminent — some very eminent ;
there are men not named there whose absence was
severe loss to the State. There were few men
better fitted to discuss questions of grave constitutional ethics than the younger (John C.) Spencer
and Gulian C. Verplanck ; and it was ever to be

regretted that the occupancy of the Governor's chair deprived the Convention of the presence of De Witt Clinton.

I do not see in that Convention that any one man ruled it. When I come to write, in pages following this, of the next constitutional gathering,— that of 1846,— I shall have but one record of fame to make there; that was Michael Hoffman's Convention,— certainly nothing less, perhaps nothing more. I can readily see that in Judge Spencer there was, in 1821, a man with all the will to rule; but there rise other names there that would not consent to any such imperialism.

Erastus Root was not a man to permit any large measure of contradiction or dictation. Mingling the roughness of pioneer life, of a semi-frontier experience, with a strong intellect, brighter than is his general reputation, he had such a vigorous will of his own, that he frequently bore down opposition without convincing it. His were the old ideas of radicalism, operating in some grandeur of theory,— waifs from the doctrines of the French revolution,— and he was in earnest. Hence, when, in after life, he found those doctrines used for selfish and petty purposes, he found it an easy thing to be enrolled among conservative men ; though in such a rank, not as distinctive or as interesting.

Certainly his earnestness did not forsake him ;

for all who witnessed, as I did in part, his senatorial career from 1840 to 1844, could not but be
amazed at the physical force with which he spoke ;
tearing his voice with a vehemence that only the
stoutest frame of lung and throat could withstand ;
and yet, with all this, there was a semi-simplicity of
character and manner about him. Of course I
allude now to his later days. I thought it a picture for a photographist to see, as I did, this veteran statesman,— his white hair and glowing face,
a velvet cap not ungracefully upon his head,—
very earnestly playing chess with a young lady;
and quite absorbed in the game he was.

Long years before that — when he was quite
another man, and, I fear I may say, a rude man —
I saw him in church rise during the sermon and
turn his back to the preacher. Perhaps that was
among the things allowed in the frontier habits to
which he was accustomed ; perhaps it was to
express his displeasure or weariness in something
which the preacher uttered. It seemed rude enough,
and I think was, at the time, the subject of comment. We have a general improvement of manners since that time. A man grieved or displeased
may, in these days, be permitted to walk out of
church, but, while in it, the law of society, as of
right is, that he must be decorous and respectful.

It was the good fortune of Erastus Root always

to appear and reappear in public life at periods of the highest interest. Perhaps it was just then that the sense of his value of public service would strongest suggest itself to the memory of his fellow-men. He was, though filling the second place, the strong man of the Executive department of 1822. He was in Congress while Jefferson was President, and while yet the storms of the last century had not subsided; in the difficult period just before and just after the war of 1812, and in the era of the nullification of 1831; in the State Senate during the war of 1812, and forty years afterward; while his service in the Assembly was scattered along from 1798 to 1830, knowing as many phases of party as Talleyrand knew of French governments. His life was a political kaleidoscope.

He requested me at one time to present him to William Lyon Mackenzie, who was then in service at Albany, as a correspondent for one of the leading New York papers. I thought it a very curious and not uncongenial nor inappropriate meeting, for both of them had sought and found the wildest waves of political agitation.

There could be something of the imaginative or poetical about his conversation. I recollect his using this figure, which I thought a beautiful one. Said he, " The mind of man is stronger after he

has passed his prime of life than at that period ;
just as the earth is warmer in the afternoon than
when the sun is in the zenith."

I attended the last day of the December term
of the Court of Errors, in 1843, knowing that it
was the completion of Erastus Root's service as of
the Senate and Court, just for the purpose of
watching the last official moment of a career so
lengthened,— beginning in 1798,— then to end ;
and the last vote he gave was on some question of
authority of the Court, and he said " No ! " and
as he was about to leave, said he, not exactly
aloud, but, as it were, aside, " This closes my
official labors for time and for eternity." I
thought then it was rather sadly or reluctantly
said. He had lived to see the fallacy of some of
his earliest and strongest views. The Erie Canal
was a national success ; yet the time had been
when the batteau-men roared by every tavern-side
on the Mohawk, at General Root's comical application to the river and the canal, of " The hole for
the big cat and another hole for the little cat, too."

A very different man — and not as eminent,
but, in his line, distinguished — was Abraham Van
Vechten, one of the Albany delegation in convention. Recollection of him cannot be effaced while
that wonderfully accurate portrait of him is in existence, which is one of the ornaments of the

room of the Court of Appeals in the Capitol. He
looked, above all other men, the personification of
the most respectable class of the old lawyer.
There was worth and integrity in his appearance
that could not be mistaken. I cannot imagine a
more pleasing, satisfactory picture than to see, as
I have seen, this aged gentleman and counsellor
sitting in the front door of his residence, or rather
of his office, at Albany, in his old-fashioned, neat,
and well-arranged costume, his Bible on his knee,
with his long pipe in mouth, and all in the quiet
appropriateness of one to whom this scene was of
the fitness of things, and so understood and accepted by all who passed. Albany had, what is so
seldom presented to popular suffrage, the difficult
choice between two most worthy men, each of
them blended with the best recollections of an
eventful period, when they had to select either
John Tayler or Abraham Van Vechten as Presidential elector.

Mr. Van Vechten was the synonyme in his
locality for safe counsel, and others beyond his
immediate neighborhood so adjudged him. Hence
John Jacob Astor selected him as one of his counsel to obtain the title of the Putnam County land,
whose romantic association with one of the early
loves of Washington is narrated in a former chapter of this volume. Although the remark was not

entirely original with him, yet it impressed me as
concentrating a large truth, when, after the publication of the Revised Statutes, he alluded to the
difficulties of finding the new enactments. " If any
one asks me," said he, " a question in common
law, I shall be ashamed if I cannot give him an
immediate answer; if he asks me of the statute
law, I shall be ashamed if I can." He *could* say
a sententious thing very cleverly. I asked him,
if he had ever been at the village of Ithaca.
" Oh, yes," said he, " all over it — in the Court
of Chancery."

Nathan Sanford was an adroit, able, over-mannered man, making the lowest bow of any man
of his time ; seeking the society of young men,
and skilful to see who those were whom he should
attach to his fortunes. He must have had all the
success he could have desired, for he filled the high
places of Chancellor and United States Senator.
He seemed to me one of those statesmen who believe in the necessity of adapting themselves to
the ways of men as they were among them, even
if the acquiescence be very insincere; but those
who knew him intimately, and yielded to his per-
suasiveness, deemed him very able, while they, even
in their allegiance to him, saw that his was a
school of statesmen, which might have congenially
included Mr. Burr.

A western county sent to that Convention a young lawyer, then, as in all his long career of public honors, a most fortunate man. Judge Nelson, then representing Cortland, was one of the two names which reappeared in the Convention of 1846. A dignified gentleman, Judge Nelson's success has been the gift of time to a most worthy recipient. We call some men fortunate, but good fortune is often only talent availing itself at once of opportunity.

When John Duer died, there was no erasure from the roll of common men. The State of New York lost of those men who were of the chief among the mighty. As a judge of one of the courts of the city of New York, he had been withdrawn from public observation. Whatever of reasoning or ability accompanied his judicial life, by that he was least known. It was to John Duer as a counsellor, as a statesman, a man of profound and clear thought, that the public ear listened for long years. I have before alluded to his reputation for eloquence, as avouched by the highest authority.

Mr. Duer believed in the wisdom that is founded upon learning, — upon the close and arduous investigation of the results at which the minds of the gifted of all ages have arrived. He came to study, as the epicurean comes to pleasure. General

Wickham, of Goshen, told me that while he was, many years since, accompanying Mr. Duer, on one of the south-western circuits, they were compelled to occupy at the tavern one room. The General, wisely believing that night was made for sleep, went to rest. Just before falling asleep, he noticed his friend standing at the bookcase, with a volume in one hand and a candle in the other. The night passed, and the morning hour came, and when he looked for Mr. Duer, he was yet at the bookcase, the book still in his grasp, and the wasted, long-wicked candle flickering in its paleness in feeble contrast with the daylight. The reader had omitted sleep; the mind had forgotten the body.

Though of the old-fashioned school of men, in the forms of courtesy and in the tastes of association, Mr. Duer was with his age always. He had no dimness of eye toward a vigorous progress. While the old wealth of classic learning was re-coined by his memory, that memory welcomed every new vein of thought.

He was of the class of men that made the city of New York remembered by every intellectual visitor. Wit, learning, eloquence, did not die with him, but they were garments that were only put off by him, as the mortal puts on immortality.

One of the greatest of the names of the Convention of 1821 remains, James Kent; and I can only regret that it never was my good fortune to meet him. But of him, there was always a high and exalted public estimate, as of the great civilian of New York's history ; and the appearance of his Commentaries was recognized as the illumination of the law, shed over it by one of the brightest minds devoted to its science. It was an era in our annals, that is, of their best pages, when this great lawyer reached his eightieth year. All that was eminent in the Bar of New York, in all parts of the State, joined in the tribute of public homage. They said, — and it was truthfully said, — " It is with the immortal Commentaries on the law of England that those on American law are now classed, and the names of Blackstone and Kent are never hereafter to be disjoined." Fortunately for James Kent, his biography is even now in preparation by one who can fully appreciate, and admirably delineate, the career of a great legal mind.

Rufus King brought to that Convention the sanction of his illustrious name, — a delegate from one of the Long Island counties ; for that section of the State could not see such an assemblage as a Constitutional Convention, without claiming to send thither its most illustrious name.

It is to the honor of New York that it placed

Mr. King in the high trust of its first senatorial representation in the forming government of the United States, and by the side of Philip Schuyler, who was so thoroughly the representative of old New York. Mr. King had just come to New York from Massachusetts. It was a noble proof that this great State had no narrow or limited views of birthright to its honors. The blended citizenship was most appropriately represented by General Schuyler and Mr. King.

I can imagine how historic Mr. King's presence in the Convention of 1821 must have been, as he had been a member of that greatest of all Conventions, that which framed the Constitution of the United States, and over which presided George Washington, who was, as Madame de Stael said of the Emperor Alexander, himself a constitution to his country. What respect must have awaited on his every movement, and with what deference to experience, gathered in schools of public service so distinguished, must his opinions have been received! I can believe all the traditions of Rufus King's ability, because I have known his son, Charles King.

Recently, Blackwood's Magazine contained an article on Harrow School, its history and its scholars; and it was mentioned that two sons of the American Minister had received education there,

11

because, so the magazine said, that gentleman had believed, that at Harrow there was less attention paid to the distinctions of rank. I doubt whether Rufus King, in giving to his sons, Charles and John A., the advantages of Harrow School, stopped to think about its rules or customs of deference to rank. They enjoyed its advantages themselves, like young gentlemen and the sons of a gentleman. It has been very interesting to me to hear their memories of boyish days when they met, in the equality of fellow-students, Byron, that greatest of poets, — but to whom the boys gave some ludicrous name for his lameness, and, for other causes, called him " the poor lord," — and Peel, so long the real ruler of England. These were associations which the future Governor of New York, the future eminent writer and scholar, do not forget ; and which form, indeed, only a brief chapter in their very interesting reminiscence.

George III. did not fail to express his satisfaction that Mr. King, while visiting Paris, was not presented to Napoleon, — " To that man," as the English monarch said of the great ruler, " by the side of whose career, history fails to remember his own." He placed the American minister's reticence in acceptable contrast with the visiting of Napoleon by Mr. Fox ; and, in his quick, nervous .

manner of repetition, said, " You did not go to see that man, — Mr. Fox did, Mr. Fox did ! "

Most of us think we could have ventured to incur the displeasure of most of the potentates of the earth, to have seen Napoleon. I recollect Mr. Gallatin expressing his regret that, in consequence of some mistaken delicacy, he did not see him while in Paris, during his service as Minister to England.

The elder Adams and the younger Adams both sent Mr. King to the English court, and he saw that central arena of earth's influences while yet the great men of the last century's power were living, and in the day of the men who had succeeded to them ; Pitt and Fox of the past, and Canning and Palmerston of the new men. It was the good fortune of Mr. King's sons to visit Charles James Fox, at his residence, and also to hear him in his place in Parliament ; and I have heard Mr. Charles King most interestingly describe the ease and quiet assurance of power with which Mr. Fox spoke, his hands reposing on his portly person.

The name connected with the Conventions of New York, that lingered longest in life, was that of John Lansing, more familiarly known as Chancellor Lansing, who led the delegation from Albany to the Convention of 1788, and who I recollect making some motion in the Supreme Court not long before his sad disappearance from among the living, and which was objected to by a lawyer, as not consistent with the practice; and the delicate and considerate manner in which the Judge — whose name, for that courtesy, I could wish to remember — said, as if deprecating the opposition, " Great allowance is to be made for the age of the counsel who has made the motion." I know I thought at the time it was a very kind scene.   '

Chancellor Lansing, with Robert Yates, gave us our only glimpse of General Washington's great Convention of 1788,— all or most of our knowledge of it, till the Madison papers were published. The Judge who was so courteous, as I have above related, was much more civil than John Sloss Hobart, one of the earliest of the judiciary, who, Judge Woodworth told me, quite sharply set *him* down, when, as a young man, he rose to address. " Sit down, young man," said he; ".nobody but a counsellor at law practises in my court ! "

Those were days when the Bench dared to say, " This is *my* court ! " and between objecting to so much individuality of power, and " reforming " it, and regretting that we had reformed quite so much, the exact place of the judiciary has not quite settled itself to this day.

Notwithstanding all that is · said — and often truly said — of the dying out of old names and old families, yet one can trace through the series of the assemblages, when the leading men of the State have been called together, a type or group of the same families from the very colonial times — indeed, into them. The Beekman and Schuyler and Clinton are familiar in 1860 as they were in 1710 and 1719 and 1743 ; and we have sent to the highest place in our State and to the Senate of the United States a descendant of the greatly misunderstood and misrepresented Stuyvesant of 1647. So our wheel of political power is not always in the guidance of new men. The name of Livingston has a lease of representation dating from the year 1777.

John C. Spencer was, emphatically, one of the first men in all the annals of New York, and, indeed, of the nation ; and it would have been uneasiness to him to have thought his name in any other than the very first line of record ; and this not of vanity, but of the consciousness of self-reliance. He asked neither pioneer nor convoy in life ; and his influence was always on the pulse of the action around him. If a *very* difficult affair was to be disentangled; if a *very* rending and racking problem of political doctrine was to be solved, men trod the very road of despair to go to his office, to find its solution. Educated and brought up amidst that illustrious school of men who circled around his father, he rose from these influences and carried away from them their best. He took study by school, by college, by grasp on learning, and by experience of the world. He brought all this to his own mould, rejecting as promptly as tamer minds acquiesced — not believing in failure, and not knowing fear.

The career of Mr. Spencer was an isolated one. He was never known as the appendage to any man. He was careful of the official proprieties of life ; but it was true of him — I know not but more truly than of any other — that whoever ruled state or nation, *did not rule him.* He was of no man's clique or cabal ; and the power that governed, whether it was by political or official influence, might, as it often did, find in him a counsellor, but it never curbed him into a vassal. What *he* believed, — his idea of the right, — he followed. Strong in his own elaborate examination, if the strength of the popular opinion flowed with his own, it was well, and he could gracefully appreciate the support ; but if it deserted him, he did not desert his judgment.

His life was a long array of service to others ; or, as it would best express the truth, of assist-ance to others. At the bar, with the rich learning

of a life-long student in the lore of the law, with
an earnestness, a seriousness of utterance that
compelled attention, he was heard by the judges
as one to neglect whose words would have been
injustice to themselves; and he could utter such
terse and forcible sentences! In the argument on
the constitutionality of the canal revenue certifi-
cate law, in 1851, in which his judgment coincided
with that of Daniel Webster, and which he regarded as one of the most important of all the
cases in which he was ever engaged, I recollect
his warning to the court, lest too often or too arbi-
trarily they should overrule or thrust aside the
effect and force of the will of the legislative branch
of the government. " Take care," said he, " the
bow, too often bent, breaks at last ! "

In the halls of legislation, he so forcibly, so
faithfully asserted a principle,— or, perhaps, oftener
combated a policy, — that, though it might be a
minority of numbers with whom he acted, it
soon became a majority of such might of argument, that the great axiom of government became
a reality in his case, " that power is always passing from the many to the few."

He held high cabinet office, and the annals of
those eminent positions, the Treasury and the War
Departments, testify of that inimitable energy,
that command over all their resources, over all

their affairs, which, in him, could only cease when the chill hand of death arrested the powers of life. His name went before the Senate of the United States, as Justice of the Supreme Court. It failed to receive their approval. That act deprived that Bench of the services of a man, before whose intellect and labor, learning and independence, the dust of decaying doubt would have been swept aside, and there would have been kept brilliant the illustrious record of Jay and Story and Marshall.

When he was but a young man, he awoke a slumbering House of Representatives to all the errors of .the financial institution of the nation, and severed and scattered every disguise which an infatuated secret organization had thrown around the terrible murder of a citizen.

There was much of the true reformer about him. He knew the distinction that exists between the radical and the reformer, and, while he scorned the ephemera that flutter to destroy, he applied the noble intellect that lived within him to make order and beauty and simplicity and right to exist where old Time had accumulated mere form or precedent or confused or costly or cumbrous forms of action.

If manuscript and type could speak, how many of the most important statutes of the land, how

many grave resolutions, how many important reports, how many lucid essays, how many earnest
editorials, uttered in the names, and issued under
the apparent ownership of others, would be found
in that neat, small, perpendicular handwriting, —
that peculiar manuscript, so condensed, so like
the work of a careful master of that great feather
in the age's cap, the pen! Labor — labor — this
was the motto of his heraldry; and he gave his
tremendous energies to the work of life, — to be
the first in whatever department of action that
labor was exercised.

It was said that he was stern and harsh. It
may be so, but I know that his were strong and
fervid sympathies and emotions. There was an
hour when, in the affair of the Somers, affliction
came upon him in its intense and most bitter form.
I have a letter of his before me, written at that
time, in which he says : " That my reason has
been preserved to me, amidst this horrible calamity,
is a source of profound gratitude."

There was a great man in action and counsel
while Mr. Spencer lived, and I could not observe
his career without this record.

With Luther Bradish went out the last light
of the last school of statesmen. In years he did
not belong to it, and is not to be classed among
them; but he was, as it were, a legacy from them

to teach us what a thorough and undeviating gentleman should do in all the dusty walks of political
life. But, superb as his manners were, and not
overwrought, when applied to the circumstances
of a parliamentary career, he was something more
and better — much more and better — than an example of courtesy. He filled only subordinate
parts. He was member of Assembly, Speaker
of the Assembly, Lieutenant-Governor, United.
States Treasurer; but it was true of him, as it was
said of a diplomat who was sent to some out-of-the-
way station, and when it was remarked that his
duties would scarcely amount to more than the
sending one letter home in a year: "But," said
his friend, "*how well he sends home that one?*"
There was no more careful and attentive and upright gentleman in all the House, speaking at the
right time, for the right thing, and clearly and
forcibly. As Speaker and as President of the
Senate, it is a proverb of the Capitol, when anything is done admirably, that it is of the school of
Luther Bradish. The nation knew, in its inmost
heart of confidence, that its treasure was safe in
his hands. Even the minor duties of life were
done so well by him. I recollect seeing him, as
one of the wardens of Grace Church, take the
collection. He offered the plate with such graceful
courtesy, as if he said to each one, " Will it,

at this time, be agreeable to you to make me the
bearer of your charities?" In truth, he was a
princely gentleman, and princes may be obliged
to me for the comparison. He gave his dignified
old age to the presidency of the noblest of all
organizations, the American Bible Society; and,
in the fitness of things, lived worthily and well, in
body and mind, till eighty years completed his
record. A charming conversationist, he had memories of the East, of Europe, of the best and
greatest; and to hear him and Henry Clay talk
together, as I have done, was a page of human
action worth a journeying to enjoy.

In a crowd of ten thousand men, Rufus Choate
would have been selected as possessing the look of
a great man. There was a grave genius about it,
which at once attracted. I saw him repeatedly,
and first, I recollect, at a party at Boston, or
rather a reception given to President Tyler, in
1843, during the furore of the festival of the laying
of the top-stone of the Bunker Hill Monument.
The collector of the port, or some other official,
had borrowed the house of a friend in which to
entertain the President; and in this crowd, Mr.
Choate mingled, greatest of all. I heard him
speak at the Baltimore presidential nominating
convention, nine years after that, 1852, when he
really wished to make one of his best speeches,

and when all the physical circumstances around him were propitious for it, — were indeed enough to make vivid the words of any man. He was put forth as the leading man of those who, at that time, sought the nomination of Mr. Webster. Though not many in numbers, they were very energetic and very zealous. I would chronicle it as contribution toward the history of the times, how zealous and energetic and devoted these men were. They desired that, amidst the almost frantic excitement of that assemblage, some one should rise, who should place Mr. Webster's right in the strongest force of words, and they chose Mr. Choate. He had the personal fitness for such a scene. Tall and self-possessed, with a commanding voice and impressive action, and all around him a crowd in earnest expectancy, either of progress toward triumph from what he should say, or of something to call forth earnest answer.

Mr. Ashmun had just read a report which embodied a declaration of principles, and there were loud cries for Choate, and he rose. He spoke with eloquence, worthy of his reputation, and was heard with applause, which in itself was worthy reward of a life of exertion. It was a superb scene. The whole convention turned to the speaker. The galleries were thronged with an

audience intently attentive, and the fervid language
of the orator found its way to their hearts. With
all his glowing eloquence, he was master of himself; and such a man is usually master of his
audience.

Though it were perhaps better introduced in
another place in this volume, I cannot omit a scene
that at that time was witnessed. Forty miles
thence, in a hotel at Washington, far away from
his beautiful Ashland, Henry Clay was on his
death-bed, close to his dying day. In his stirring
life he had often received ovations of praise for
word and service, enough to wreath the richest
laurel that ever fell on the head of man; but
never, in all his brilliant career, did brighter lustre
shine on his name, than when Governor Jones
pointed to his portrait, and the response was given,
— such a response as seemed the concentration of
the people's pulse of joy.

I saw Mr. Choate when he was a member of
the Massachusetts Constitutional Convention, — a
body which ought to have attracted to it the attention of all who have pleasure in an intellectual
gathering, but which, as not including Everett
and other great names of Massachusetts, did not
present a thorough representation. I recollect
by what a weary staircase we found our way to
the place of observation, — a long staircase with

interminable succession of steps, with little, narrow, inquisition-like ranges of seats. One ought
to have heard the richest of language to compen-
sate. Mr. Choate was not speaking, but listening.
He did that well. He listened very attentively to
Governor Marcus Morton, who was demonstrating
that thereafter there ought to be no Council around
the Governor of Massachusetts, but that he ought
to stand alone. Doubtless his argument was good,
but it failed to convince Mr. Choate, for, attentively as he listened, he voted against the ex-
governor's proposition. Amidst that convention
he sat, *the* man of mark. I doubt whether, in all
the history of his life, as looked at from the close,
he was fortunate or wise in having left the arena
of the bar for that of the statesman. In and about
the law, in the practice of its highest tribunals,
and the true argument of its greatest problems, he
was creating, indeed had created, a name for himself of the first celebrity ; and it would have been
greater fame to have been recognized as head of
the American lawyers, rather than to have been
known as foremost friend even of Daniel Webster.

In that very beautiful belt of land, which is
about all that the State of New York has preserved to the Indian, — a mere pathway by the
forming waters of the Alleghany, — the man who

best deserves record and remembrance was the old
chief Blacksnake, a very unprepossessing name,
and, in justice to the Indians, perhaps would sound
better to us if we could but master the syllables,
so short and disconnected, by which they knew
him. He was a wonderful man, if only for his
age; for even in all the doubts of all great claims
to longevity, it seemed in proof that he had passed
the hundred by several years. Those three figures of life! How few see them, how very few
see them, in possession of anything that gives life its
value! The greater part of those whose eyes behold the beauty of this world, see, before their age
needs enumeration by more than one figure, the
glories of a better. He was said to be more than
one hundred and eight years old. I suspect it will
be well to add the qualifying words, of a conveyance of real estate, " be the same more or less."
His life connected the majesty and misery of the
Indians' history. He was a living man when, in
these States, the Indian was a nation so powerful
that its alliance was sought; and, what was much
more practical, its power was feared ; and that life
lingered on till the Indian became a forgotten word
of the white man — his estate a mere reservation,— his existence dimly known to the people.
He took part in the battle of Wyoming,— a battle,
with its incidents, made immortal in the genius of

Campbell, who had faint ideas of Indian or of Susquehanna Valley.

Blacksnake was of singular beauty of form, and would have been the object of great attention, if he had gone beyond the limits of the land where was the home of his old age; but he bore his retirement with dignity, and, of his people, he was almost as much alone as the pines in the modern forest.

The Iroquois keep up the forms of their old confederacy yet, though it is but the plaid of the clan. They have their intricacies and policy, and the chief, the Atoharho, must yet be of a particular tribe, and of a special family of that tribe. So the Henry IX., the last Stuart, without any other appendage of a sovereignty, except a disputed title, and a pitying pension, believed himself the true king; and amidst falling and failing races, something of the old lives to make unhappy the obscurity of the present. Few men, peer or peasant, can divest themselves of the idea that something of the past gives them worth, however unrecognized.

A few Indians, known to me, had made the history of their own people their study. Like as among the Jews, in their captivity, the memories of their brighter day lived and glowed amidst their bondage; so do the traditions of the past dominion exist among the Iroquois; and there are legends and narratives, not of course in books, — for what but the bark of the birch tree was their papyrus? — but, as of old, uttered from the aged to the young, complete access to which these doubly intelligent men alone possessed.

I once said to one of these gentlemen,— for, with all their life, they possessed the manners of gentlemen,— " I can understand what you, an educated man, do with yourself in the long winter evenings, for you can do just what we do, with books ; but what *do* your people, who are not educated, as you are, do with themselves ? " " They," said he, " oh, they sit around the fire and tell stories."

And this is type of the Oriental,— of all those who have social intercourse without books ; hence the vast majority of the history of the world, however little of it may reach us, is of and by, tradition.

The most ludicrous instance of civilization among them that I noticed, was, while the pageant of the opening of the Erie Railway was passing through the Reservation, to see an Indian in the sunshine with an umbrella over his head,— the delicacy of his complexion probably being in danger !

It is but a few years since one of these Indian

12

gentlemen indicated how well he could use the
mystic, figurative language of his ancestry, by the
following letter of invitation to an Indian gathering, which he sent to me:

" *My dear Friend,*— The great A-to-har-ho, of the Onondaga Nation of the Iroquois Confederacy, has been here bear
ing a wampum, which he directed me to send to the western
door of the Long House.

" The message which the wampum bore was, that the
Grand Sachem is about to take the ashes off the embers of
the Council Fire of the Iroquois, and that each member of
the Grand Council must watch the East, to see the smoke of
the Council Fire as it first emerges from the tops of the
forest.

" Each ear must be listening daily in order to hear the
footsteps of the next messenger, who will bring the string
with the knots denoting the number of nights which shall
supervene before the convocation of the Grand Council.

" The Council will be held at the residence of the Keeper
of the Council Fire at Onondaga. It will be held within a
month, when all the wampums of the Iroquois Confederacy
will be brought out, and the traditions repeated, according to
the ancient customs of the confederacy."

The day in which our lot is cast will not be dissevered in personal association from the Indian,
but it will see him only as one sees an old picture,
torn and defaced and marred. Not that he was ever,
except in few instances, the Roman " stoic of the
woods," as he has been called. He was a man of

few ideas, few resources. It was a theory of
Henry R. Schoolcraft, who had made their history his special study, that the Indian, residing
amidst the recesses of the forest, believed in a
special mythology of the woods,—not so much the
Pan and Dryad, as some sterner deities or phan-
toms; and it was through fear of them that he
was a silent man ; his vocabulary was limited by
his dread of the unseen.

I have had an Indian pour into my hearing, in
low and musical voice, the tradition of the creation
of the several tribes of the Iroquois, — the reve-
lation that dispersed the original people, and their
wanderings,— a blending of the wild and the gro-
tesque, but, as of the ways of a decaying race,
very interesting,— legends, in which incidents of
a historical character, and the groundwork of
which is adopted by us in our annals, mingled with
stories that seemed childish even for the red man.

I remember when, after some fierce outbreak in
the then Far West, it was deemed politic, by the
government, to show a delegation of the Menom-
inees what the physical greatness and power of
the Atlantic States was, and these men came
down State street in a post-coach. They were
powerful men, in a degree that gave us just idea
of what their strength and force were in their pri-
mal day.

John Miller, of Truxton, an eminent physician, to whom I have before alluded, in that part of this volume illustrating Washington, told me that he was seated in the gallery of the House of Representatives, when his attention was given to the occurrence of a young person engaged in conversation with the Speaker. From his boyish look, he presumed him to be one of the pages of the House. The interview was a brief one, but it was historic in the annals of Congress. It was when John Randolph presented himself to take the constitutional oath of office, on being elected member of the House; and when the presiding officer asked him — of course, in pleasantry — whether he was of the age defined by the Constitution, and Randolph said, "Ask my constituents."

The spectator of the scene long outlived the Virginian orator. What an orator! He could talk for hours of nothing, and talk so well, so beautifully, that it poured over the memory as the quick, glittering water pours over the agate-strewn bed of Minnesota's streams, indicating the precious stone, but not bearing it on. He was of those who seemed, by instinct, to know the affairs over whose elaborate workings other men must toil long before they obtain analysis — who was a cyclopædia in knowledge — who had eye to see the beautiful and tongue to talk it.

CHAPTER V.

OME of the incidents I have narrated in these pages I gathered from the conversation of Josiah Quincy, whose life extended from about 1772 to 1860. When he wrote in his old age, at a period when most men have their energies taxed to keep their intellect together, the life of John Quincy Adams, I thought it was a question of doubt which was most interesting, the biography or the biographer. He was of Boston when learning was a rare thing in the republic and yet found home in Harvard; and when yet the old-fashioned families of the colonial times moved on in brocaded form. Lord Lyndhurst's father, thought he had sold some lots in Beacon street too cheaply, and made inquiry afterward; but Mr. Copley found that he had discovered the value of property in Boston too late. Had his earlier judgment been master of the situation, he would have been richer for his old estate in the "rebel-

(181)

lious Town of Boston." Lord Lyndhurst and
Mr. Quincy — associates in childhood — saw the
great volume of life and history open its strongest
pages.

When Josiah Quincy was in Congress, the day
of fierce conflict of principle was in zenith fervor,
and he walked in the heat without a shade. They
who took the power knew his strength, whether
the blow was on their armor or for their cause.
For him to write the history of such a statesman
as was Mr. Adams, was as if Rossini should write
the history of Music. I once saw Mr. Quincy
standing by the base of Franklin's statue, and
wished a photographist had turned the gaze of the
sun where my own was.

The last public address I heard from him was
in that grand gathering of intellectual men, which
made so memorable the Triennial Meeting of the
Alumni of Harvard College in 1858. I cannot forget it. Mr. Winthrop presided; at his side was
Mr. Quincy, Lord Napier, the then Minister from
England, Edward Everett, Charles King, Motley,
the historian, Felton, the man to whom Harvard
entrusted safely its classics, Mr. Holmes, and a
long line of agreeable and remarkable people.

Far advanced beyond the fourscore which our
years reach only by reason of strength, Mr. Quincy
was not merely by his former association with the

college, but by the great fact of his mental and
physical power, the most remarkable of all that
rare group, and his speech was worthy of the
event. I know that in its sequence he gave me
the opportunity of proving, what indeed I had
not then for the first time to learn, the readiness
of Mr. Everett, in the immediate answer or adaptation to a quick call upon him, for reply. Mr.
Quincy alluded to the interesting recollection that
sixty years before that day, when, said he, the
orator who has so delighted you this morning
(Mr. Everett had made the great College address
of the Commencement), was but three years old ;
he (Mr. Q.), had in that hall pronounced a discourse. When, a brief period afterward, Mr. Everett rose to speak, said he, " My age has been
somewhat suddenly alluded to by the venerable
Ex-President of the College, while he was telling
you that sixty years had elapsed since his address
was here spoken. Now I wish to say to him and
to you, gentlemen, that the only reason why I was
not in this hall to hear *that* address, was because I
was *but* three years old."

On this occasion (1858), it seemed to me that
it would be difficult, anywhere else in America, to
have gathered such a collection of men whose
spoken or written words, had made greater impression on the age in which they lived. Mr.

Quincy's rising was met by an unrestrained, almost boisterous, welcome from the crowd of educated men who filled the hall. They were moved, swayed, delighted, instructed, counselled, by the clear and wise words the aged man uttered. We felt as if the great Past had arisen from its ashes into its old fire.

I saw Mr. Quincy last, at one of the earlier meetings of the Union Club of Boston, in December, 1863. On entering the rooms in the house which was formerly the residence of Abbott Lawrence, the first and most interesting group 1 witnessed was that of Mr. Quincy, looking very aged and infirm, in conversation with Mr. Everett. He was the object of the most affectionate respect by all gathered there, and as he slowly and almost painfully walked into the supper-room, it was evident that we saw the closing shadows of that long and memorable life.

And this man, so much a man of skill in words and literature, which are not supposed to be especially in alliance with the practical, added very largely to his fortune by his sagacity and financial courage ; by seeing what others did not or would not see, and by taking a risk from which others turned, and about which they made warning, after he was eighty years of age ! Had he not abundant other material about him for a good and true fame, this would win the world's attention. I knew another gentleman in another city, a private citizen, who lost a large fortune after he had arrived at the same far advanced period of life, and who took his loss calmly. It went beyond the hundred thousand, and had every possible circumstance of annoyance except the one great fact that *his* integrity was not questioned. He lived to see himself again classed among wealthy men. After eighty years of age, how few there are that would meet quietly great gain or loss. It illustrates the comparative longevity of ancient and modern times, that it is at this very age — fourscore — that Barzillai excused himself from acceptance of King David's welcome to the court at Jerusalem, by declaring that with him the senses had refused to recognize or know the touch of luxury or the voice of harmony.

The great age of Mr. Quincy, with his known association with the councils of the nation at such remote period, made him, I think, at his death, the most remarkable of all our public men. We hear of such aged public men in England, but find very few of them in our own land of greater frost and hotter sun.

Henry Clay, of all men in whose pathway in life I ever found myself, I saw so often, heard in such variety of speech and conversation, that I find in my own reminiscence that which, if it

should not interest my readers, has been to myself
a delight in its reawakening.   He was so distinctly the leader of men, wherever he went, whatever he did,— so broadly and boldly did it show
itself, so vivid was he as he moved, and so fascinating as he talked, so potent as he spoke,— that we
all saw at once that, while he belonged to us in
the birthright of country, he would have been, in
any country of civilization, of its masters ; and all
this he possessed, all this he displayed, and it stood
out from him, while he was almost at all times the
political head but of a minority of the people.   It
was the supremacy of the individual, of the man in
and of himself,— not accreting to himself station,
but something which, now that we look at in the
results of the years, we can see was more enduring
than any station.   His name is of the household
names of the nation, while it is sometimes necessary to refresh our memory by the aid of statistics
as to the roll of Presidents ; yet he, with all his
greatness, never saw that.   He could not, or
would not, see that the enthusiastic, the disinterested friendship, the loyalty shown toward him,
was greater honor, greater reward than the certifi-
cate of Electoral Colleges.

I first saw Mr. Clay when he was on a tour
through Western New York, and when he made a
brief stay at Auburn.   That he would probably be

there on the day named, had been communicated far and wide, and those hurried thither who could. It was in the time of the coaches of Sherwood, and the supremacy of turnpikes. The cortege moved slowly, as we should read the word slow at this day, though in its own time quite surely and with progress. An enthusiastic procession, self-arranged, of men devoted to him, were at his side, having adhered to him in his welcomings at the line of villages through which he had passed. It was a hot day, and the dust had risen to look at the orator. With all that could be done by the best-hearted and most liberal friends, it was yet a toilsome ride. But to hear and see him, that crowd had come; and giving him, as I thought, brief respite to get rid of the choking dust, he was called to a staging erected at the American Hotel; and then I first saw him, tall, not graceful (except when the magic of his voice had won you to believe no man else could be as graceful), hard in features, but with a look and way that at once revealed the man that knew no superior.

He seemed to have had no time given him for preparation to speak. Indeed, it seems to me now as if the dust was on him. He was formally and rather ponderously addressed by a leading citizen of Auburn (Mr. Bronson), and Mr. Clay listened with all dignity and orderly patience; the

crowd would have preferred brevity. He replied
ever so admirably. Though this was but a way-
side, unstudied speech, it is not forgotten to this
day, and some of his gestures were themes of
especial admiration. Of course his address was,
after pleasant words of gratitude for the welcome
given him, concerning the prevalent political
themes, and therefore evanescent, but at the hour
it made the deepest impression. He delineated
the discipline with which the party opposed to him
moved. " At the word of command, if need be,"
said he, " they ground their arms ; " and here he
dropped his hat, which he had held in hand.
Of course, how this hat was to be recovered by
him, without some very awkward movement, by a
man so tall, was to all of us an object of special
wonder ; but in the same figure, and in the delineation of some other process in the movement of a
thoroughly ordered army, his long arm swept
gracefully down, and in the fitness of the words
used, so that it seemed precisely appropriate, the hat
was regained. That occasion rejoiced the whole
country around, and is yet memorable. Soon after,
he went to the belvidere on the top of the American,
from whence the view is of a large area of wealthy
and well-cultured land. He enjoyed this. Just about
that time, the leading topic of political conversation
was the speech of Wm. C. Rives, of Virginia, who

had spoken somewhat laudatory of his (Mr. Rives') farm of five thousand acres, at Castle Hill. Mr. Clay, looking somewhat disdainfully, making the gesture, in him always so expressive,— the stretching out his arm,— said, as he looked at the beautiful farms that lay almost beneath him, " I would not give one thousand acres of this land for all his five thousand at Castle Hill."

He seemed to me, as I saw him alone, not animated. It may have been the fatigue, or it may have been of his characteristic, to illuminate only under the influence of numbers around him. His use of snuff seemed to me immoderate. Since Scott, in that delightful book, the Pirate, makes the poet of Burgh Weston, Claud Halcro, to rejoice, as a choice reminiscence, that he filled the snuff box of " glorious John Dryden," I am not sure but that a similar service to the statesman is " not to be sneezed at."

In the evening a reception was given him at the residence of Governor Seward, and there he was in high state of animation, delighting men as he ever did. I recollect one remarkable expression which he used. He was alluding to one of the occasions on which his name had been in the Presidential canvass. " I received," said he, " a tremendous defeat; but my measures, my measures all triumphed ! "

I believe I next saw him at Albany, in the City

Hall, addressing the young men, and acknowledg-
ing the gift of a superb blue cloth cloak, which became his form admirably.   I remember the exultation with which the man who made it stood by and
saw the affair.   I am sorry to have to record that
that superb garment was stolen from Mr. Clay a
few days afterward ; a circumstance which, I think,
he ought to have considered as, at least, among the
lesser griefs of his chequered destinies.

Years passed on, and he had been candidate
for the Presidency in 1844,— a year whose history
might be written, a most interesting chapter in our
political annals.   That is not for this volume.
Suffice it to say, that it was distinguished by a
personal devotion never before given in this country to any man, and never since — losing the characteristics of a political adherence in the grander,
though perhaps less sagacious, attributes of loyal
fidelity.   More men worked and voted for Mr.
Clay in that year *disinterestedly,*—just because
they were for him above and outside of all other
considerations,— than the annals of this country
record in case of any other man.   It was a personal
attachment, as intense as that of the Highlanders
to Prince Charlie.

But all this is out of the intent of this work.
He had grown older, and vicissitudes had left their
mark upon his frame ; but when he entered Syra-

cuse, a guest of the New York State Agricultural
Society, the grand old man was in all his individual power over all around him. And all over the
State, the attraction of travel toward the State
Fair became potent, as the word spread everywhere that Henry Clay was to be there. His name
had, as the old Scotch ballad sings, " music in it."

Mr. Clay's reception at the State Agricultural
Fair held at Syracuse, in 1849, was of those chapters in life which he who reads cannot forget, nor
is this forgotten. It is the chosen, cherished recollection of many hearts, for it combined the incidents of a widely enthusiastic welcome unto one
who, though he held neither station nor power,
was regarded by all as worthy of all they could
do or could say for him and to him. No vision of
future gift or grant or place gilded this reception.
It was the Americanization of the loyalty which in
other days and countries clung around the Stuart —
was faithful to the death to name and lineage.

Syracuse, a busy and advancing city, reversing
the fate that befell the disobedient wife of old time,
turning itself from salt to life, was thronged; rail
and road and canal had exhausted all their facili-
ties in bringing together THE PEOPLE, from the hour
that it was known Henry Clay was to be there.
He had been specially invited by the officers of
the society, at whose head were John A. King,

afterward Governor of the State, and Benjamin P. Johnson, the man who, beyond all others, has rendered highest service to the agriculture of the country. Mr. Clay had accepted the invitation, and playfully remarked, as he consented, " I shall be the biggest ox on the ground."

The Fair soon became the picture of the one man and of the crowd,— of a vast mass of intelligent, independent men, giving themselves gladly to the watch around him, to cheer him, to talk of him, to rally around him, and in their own good-hearted, enthusiastic way, utterly to defeat all his purposes of looking at the incidents and collections of the Fair. It was the welcome of rural New York to Henry Clay, and all else was forgotten : all else remembered was blended in some way with that.

His arrival was the great event of the day. The station was circled by a crowd whose enthusiasm, when he did come, would heed no restraint. The barouche, in which he was conveyed to the home prepared for him, could with difficulty find way ; the stirring, energetic voice of Governor King was exerted to make itself heard in the tumult, as he begged them to give a road for the gallant Harry. I so well recollect this scene. Mr. Clay was of all men most fitted for such incidents, for he had a word of kindness or courtesy or wit for all.

It was in vain for him to attempt a careful scrutiny of the exhibition. The crowd allowed no such thing. They massed around him, and wherever he went, it was their most sovereign pleasure to accompany him. From tent to tent, from sheep to oxen, from implement to picture, if Mr. Clay desired to see, that desire must yield to the greater, of being seen. I recollect being near him as a daguerreotype of himself (for the advance to photography was not yet) was brought out to the carriage and shown to him. Instantly he saw it he said, so wittily, " Horribly like me ! " Everywhere in the street, or in the Fair grounds, was this enthusiasm shown, till I heard him say, "Well, gentlemen, let us go home ; we can do that, when we can do nothing else."

At his lodging, it was necessary, in regard to his peace, and in reference to preserving him unharmed amidst the storm of kindness, to establish a friendly quarantine, and not to permit an indiscriminate entrance. The claims for a special interview were sometimes touching in their devotion. Men who lived afar off, and in districts where the vast preponderance of political opinion had been always against Mr. Clay, and they alone had kept his flag flying,— such men begged that they might go in to see him ; for it was to see him that their journey had been made, and to speak with him

13

was the reward of a lifetime. They were admitted, and they were recompensed.

Mr. Webster once said, " I would like to know what sort of people are your people of Western New York, that they are so devoted to Mr. Clay ? "

But this crowd would not be content with seeing him. They *must* hear that voice, whose music had been the harmony of the nation in a career of eloquence. They were determined to hear him speak, and so they besieged the doors, blocked up the windows, kept all the fresh air out, until some of his considerate and merciful friends suggested that he should satisfy the desire of the people by a brief address. He proceeded to the north balcony of the Syracuse House; and around the house the eager crowd gathered itself, wildly welcoming the grand old man as he stepped in front,and, with the already kindling eye, looked out on the multitude of *friends* — yes of friends. He had no office to give, no place to promise. He was never to be anything more or higher than he had been. The welcome to him was to the powerless, but it was the proudest that could form the voice of fame. I recollect at the time being delighted with the speech, as up to his reputation. Indeed, in my experience of his oratory, I think that was of the most attractive. He alluded to his being an old man, gray-headed, worn out. But when he said

that, the crowd denied: "No, no! you are good
for fifty years yet." He said (I do not believe he
meant this) that· he had hoped to have passed
through the State quietly, unobserved, unrecognized; and here again the cry met him, "*You
can never do that.*"

Said he : " When I go back to Kentucky, I expect to attend an agricultural fair there. My
friends will crowd around me, and they will say to
me, ' O Mr. Clay, you have been at the great
State Fair of New York. Come, tell us all about
it, — tell us of the Devons, and the Durhams, and
the Herefords.' And I shall tell them, ' I saw no
Devon, I saw no Durham, no Hereford. I saw
nothing ' " — and here he· used that great circle
of a gesture, which only his arm could effect in
grace, — " ' I saw nothing but *the people.*' "

All this was a scene not to be obliterated. The
young city would be reluctant to lose it from its
annals. It left its traces in the memories of men,
who, to this hour, as they will to their latest, preserve it, as the owner of precious stones his treasures.

The city was more than crowded. It was over-
flowing, — it was saturate with people. All the
devices of remunerated entertainment and generous hospitality were poured forth. In Mr. Clay's
suite were the Vice President, Mr. Filmore, Gov-

ernor Hamilton Fish, Mr. King, Mr. Granger, the brave old soldier, Solomon Van Rensselaer, all exulting in the welcome given to their chief.

Some of my readers may say to themselves, " Is this warm portraiture of the progress of Mr. Clay real, or is it colored by a partisan feeling ? " I think I can answer them, that I have written this historically, in the wish to convey, if I can, a just idea of the feeling that existed toward this extraordinary man. His personal fascination was irresistible. Faults, deep and grievous, he indeed had. His life *had* written lines, which, dying, he might wish to blot. There *were* fractures and flaws in the line of light. To my thought, it was always painful that Mr. Clay did not hear the clarion sound of his own fame; that it was far above the temporary shout to the political victor of the day ; that to him was accorded the greatest of all rewards, — the disinterested love of men.

Well, if the people of Western New York were, as Mr. Webster thought, strangely attached to Mr. Clay, let us palliate it by the reflection that he wielded over all men authority by a power, which is a gift so rarely bestowed upon men, that its record comes to us in history only as the illuminated letter in the missal, at the head of chapters, and those chapters do but symbolize centuries. Remember, too, that Mr. Clay possessed the glamour, not only in the public address, glowing and glittering in the light of an admiring audience, but in his conversation, in that way by which he took the hearts of men, even while their judgment refused to go with their hearts. Even analyzed, true feeling will not grow cold. Governor Seward admirably said that Mr. Clay held the key which fitted the wards of every man's heart.

But whoever wished *not* to be fascinated by Mr. Clay must not have encountered him in the brilliancy of social intercourse. There he was of that rarest class of men, whose conversation is a delight, and yet Mr. Clay was not a learned or accomplished man. He could not quote the classics in correctness. He knew so little of music, that when, at the ratification of the Treaty of 1814–15, the authorities at Ghent wished to serenade the American Commissioners by their national air, the application for its score was made in vain both to Mr. Clay and Mr. Adams, and all that enabled the band of the Flemish city to acquit themselves successfully in Yankee Doodle was that Mr. Clay's colored servant whistled it for the leader.

But Mr. Clay had something in conversation that was in the place of study and of music, — he had the indescribable manner that at once enthralled. It was the glamour of his way, — it was fascination.

Mr. Phœnix of New York, then residing in one

of the houses near the Battery, gave Mr. Clay a superb entertainment. It was, I believe, in the very last visit which he ever made to New York. The dinner-party included Governor Bradish, Dr. Wainwright, and other gentlemen, with a brilliant representation of ladies.

Mr. Clay entered the drawing-room with a presence that at once attracted every one to his observation. A tall, old man, in the years near the threescore and ten, his step and tread was like that of a sovereign. He came in with an impressive manner that would, in another man, have been sensational. In him, it was so graceful in all its grandeur, that it gratified while it absorbed us; and, from that moment to the hour when he took his leave, no one but himself was in the thought or attention of all. He had no rival, not even with the very agreeable young ladies who were present, and who, with just appreciation, found, of all men, this homely old man the most delightful.

Yes, this homely old man, — for the physical features of Mr. Clay's face were hard and forbidding, but the picture needed only the light to reveal it. His thought and word soon made that face the one to which all concentrated gaze.

He was in admirable spirits, talked with animation, illustrated whatever subject was presented to him, and enjoyed everything, pleasantly par-

ticipating in the abundant hospitality, and at the
close of the dinner complimenting his host as only
Mr. Clay could have done.   The day previous he
had dined with Stephen Whitney.   "Mr. Phœnix,"
said he, " when I think of this superb dinner you
have given me to-day, and the equally elegant
dinner I enjoyed with Mr. Whitney yesterday, I
am not sure, sir, but that it is my duty immediately I take my seat at Washington to propose a
sumptuary law."

He seemed to take it very kindly that one of the
guests had recently read and remembered an argument he had made in the Supreme Court of the
United States, and would at intervals allude to it
in the course of the evening.   Probably he believed it was only his political speeches that men
would read.

I recollect Mr. Bradish asked him who was the
Henry Adams, whose name appears with the other
British commissioners, at Ghent.   " Oh, Henry
Adams," said he, " he was a dry equity lawyer."

He considered Earl Gray to have been the most
eloquent man whom he heard in the English debates.

But it is not by fragments of his conversation
that I remember that occasion so well.   It was the
one pervading effect of his irresistible manner, —
not at all guarded, nor yet boisterous, but with
such heartiness, such strength all the while, and.

so utterly different from that of all other men, —
that his influence became a stream which like the
fairy view impelled you to go with it; and while
I do not recollect all that he said, the effect was
too vivid to pale with the retreating years.

And he could keep up this brilliant festive way.
Returning from the dinner, he went to the house
whose hospitalities had been offered to and accepted by him, the residence of Egbert Benson,
in Warren street, — a thoroughfare not then, as
now, devoted to business. Here it had been arranged to give to him a serenade, and accordingly
in a short time a great crowd of gentlemen, with
one of the selected bands of· New York, were
gathered around the door. If a great crowd in
the night in the streets of a city is a mob, then
never has New York seen so selected a mob. It
was his eager, anxious, devoted friends, and he
had neither place nor office to bestow. Mr. Ull-
man was the master of the ceremony, and he con-
jured the crowd to be calm. "Have patience, gentlemen," said he, "have patience, and you shall
see the idol of your souls." Meanwhile, amidst the
darkness, but a few lights shone, — for there was
none of the sensational accompaniments of pyro-
techny, — the music so exquisitely played, the air
we all knew so well in 1844, — "Here's to you,
Harry Clay;" after some time the hall-door

opened, and with friends at his side, holding large
astral lamps, so that he could be distinctly and
most picturesquely seen, Mr. Clay advanced, and
then the almost midnight air rung with the cheers
of heart-given voice. The acknowledgment was
rapturously received. When he paused, there were
cries for him to proceed. " You cry, go on," said
he; "that is easy for *you* to say, but where am I
to get the ammunition?" All these words, it may
be, look tame enough on paper, but in that scene,
said as he said them, and heard as we heard them,
they were electric. That sweet serenade ceased,
and the gratified gentlemen dispersed, and I believe as Mr. Clay's form faded into the hall, it
was the last I ever saw of that wonderful man, to
whom above all others I felt what must be meant
by the word, loyalty, — the willingness to do all
for him with only the reward of the pleasure of
having so done. When next I was near him, it
was when he was a dying man at a hotel in Washington. President he never was, but Ruler he
always was.

Several years after Mr. Clay died, I found, being
at Cincinnati, that the completion of the Covington and Lexington railroad placed within the easy
control of a few hours' journey, Lexington, a
city near which most of the private life of Mr.
Clay had been passed, and which will ever remain

of the deepest interest to every one who is grateful that his country produced such a man, and most of all to those whose best energies were given to his fortunes, and who feel that the hour which took him from the field of politics removed the only man that in this century possessed the personal, disinterested love of a great number of the American people, — a joy in him, which was to him a devotion, the like to which none other man on this side the Atlantic ever woke in the people. Lexington, as containing in its vicinage Ashland, would have been fit pilgrimage, even in the days of coach and turnpike, — how much more now when the car, with the comfort of a parlor and the speed of a bird, is the transit!

To reach the Covington Road is the difficulty and the dilemma of the journey. Snugly as to the appearance, the streets of Cincinnati and Covington fit each other, when one comes to test the union of these lines, the deep valley of the river changes the affair materially. To accommodate this fluctuating Ohio River, — this alternation of a deep deluge and moist sand, — the broad inclined plane remains without any line of street. The descending omnibus was shaken and tossed, and quivering on the line of balance that tested the tenure of the four wheels, its passengers found the passage a very rough one, and we listened kindly and approvingly to the promises of a suspension bridge, which should end all such* adventurous climbings.

The road once gained, brought us safely and easily and smoothly through a rich country, to the steadfast, solid, and respectable old city of Lexington, so called because the companions of Daniel Boone heard in their far-off wilderness exploration of the eventful hour which at the Lexington of Massachusetts opened the great gate of modern progress.

We saw Kentucky field and forest, — the former glowing in a depth and richness of verdure that seemed the very gala day of the spring, and the latter in a glory of great trees, each in its own strength and height, scattered in such varied beauty of position as would have thrilled Downing's heart, and each as clear of underbrush as though the forest had been the park.

At Lexington we drove to the Phœnix hotel, and at its portal the landlord met us like a stout host of the olden time.

" We reached the hall-door where the charger stood near."

He was there to welcome us, and in a way of hearty, genial manner, that had associations of the Tabard and of Chaucer. We soon made arrangement for going to the place which was the heart of our journey, Ashland. We found Lexington old-fashioned and rather quiet, but with a look of good order. It was soon passed through, and a ride of about a mile brought us to the place, which at least, while this generation remains, will be a household word. I did not expect to find Ashland so near the city. I thought that Mr. Clay when he spoke of his neighbors in the city of Lexington, took the word in the large-spaced sense, in which rural gentlemen speak of those who live in their vicinage. The pleasant old city may, in the changing fortunes of time, decay and fade, but its suburb secures it a place in history. The landlord told us that it was Mr. Clay's invariable practice to go home from the city at twelve o'clock.

Our carriage was driven up a short avenue, and as we alighted, there was an immediate contest of feeling between the practical and the thoughtful. The old house, the Ashland, as it was the residence of the home-life of Henry Clay, was gone. A new, well-built, handsome mansion was in its place, — and that of itself anywhere would be attractive. It had the plan, the outside look, the form in body and wings, of the house to which the heart had been pilgrimage, but

"He's not the true king for a' that."

It was not the house of Henry Clay. Of course

the owner had the right to manage the estate as
his judgment counselled ; yet I think he owed it to
such a father to let that house stand while beam
and rafter would bind. It might burn down, blow
down, crush in or crumble out,— that would have
been the same touch of time that effaces all things ;
but the nation did ask, did hope that the house
whence Henry Clay had so often departed on mission of eloquent word and statesman act, would
remain. The superb grounds of Ashland provided many most eligible situations for new and
luxurious dwellings. It would have been but kind
to the friends of Mr. Clay to have given the old
house to alternate storm and sunshine for the years,
as they were on the silver-voiced old man. But
the regrets were vain. The house of association
was off the land and this elegant new one was in
its place.

Thanks to that man who invented the words
real estate, the soil could not be taken away. In
all its matchless beauty of tree and lawn and field
and glade and garden, Ashland existed, more
lovely than our hope or thought of it had created,
and just such a surrounding of the lovely as could
instruct in its symbol language the tongue of the
orator. These were the earth-written memories
of Henry Clay. It was in this delightful scenery
that his home-life had passed. This land was his

home. It cannot be changed, and, once seen, is not to be forgotten. The residents of the house were absent, but the courtesy of the attendants permitted us to wander over the lawns and take closer look at the superb trees. As we were not invited to the garden by any proper authority, we did not bear away any floral souvenir, but we secured some of the grasses and some ash, out of which the cunning of the graver should fabricate some memorial of the day. In this soil I could see some reason for the ardent home-love which has so distinguished the people of this State.

A bright, manly little fellow rode up the lawn on his black pony. It needed but a glance at his face, and the resemblance was so apparent, so truthful, so much like *him*, that we at once exclaimed, " The Mill-Boy of the Slashes!" The incident was delightful. It was looking back upon a page of closed time, with a truthfulness which we cannot forget. I have seldom seen such accuracy of resemblance as this grandson bore to his illustrious lineage.

We found the space allotted by that resistless fate, the railway's time-table, too short, for Ashland grew upon our liking. It had, in its natural features, all we could have asked for it to furnish us in confirmation of the mind's picturing. A place it was to which a statesman might go to reinvigorate the mind chafed by the strife of the patriot in the struggle of that contest that ever will be between the noble-hearted and the untrue.

We took from the gates of Ashland the keenest regret that the views of the country and of the proprietor of the estate could not have harmonized in the preservation of the house, but consoled to our very heart by the conviction that the fields and flowers and trees, *he* had loved so well, had perpetual home of beauty.

And now, when the scale of just discrimination of his worth, just appreciation of his power, just estimate of his genius comes to that fair poise when history makes up the record, the shadows of calumny and opposition and wrong, that once were so dense around him, are breaking away. We must moderate our fear of present injustice by remembering that truth is a distant magnet, but it is a sure one. It will draw to it the right and the honorable. Let every public man remember that, to his earthly career, something of the great rule of Christian conduct belongs. It is the far-off end that makes the quiet of the present hour. It was the middle of the nineteenth century before Macaulay rose to enshrine in its truth the man and the results of the Revolution of 1688.

The grandeur of Mr. Clay's public service somebody will yet be found truly to delineate ; and so,

in writing of his home, we take up the old refrain,
" Here's to you, Harry Clay!" ·

There must have been something of the prophetic
in Washington Irving's thought when he gave to
his home, on the eastern shore of the Hudson, the
appellation of Sunnyside; for, so far as we see,
who only judge by the surface, it was a pleasant and a prosperous abiding-place ever; and the
judgment of the transient observer seems confirmed by the record of his life, as his biographer
has memorialized it.   Yet he won it after years,
many years of cares and of vicissitudes, and the
Sunnyside of the river was that to which he, like
almost all other men, attained only after crossing
the agitated and troubled tide.

I had some opportunities of personally observing
him, and had the good sense to know that they
were worthy of being improved, as far as good
manners would permit.   His early writings flowed
into the genial, thoughtful, ideal life of literature
which was forming under the influences of the
Waverley books, leading men to look at the old
time through the exquisite veil which intellect was
weaving over it.   Mr. Irving took the dwellings
of the past, and declining to people them, as did
Mrs. Radcliffe, with spectres, who made the days
hideous and the nights uncomfortable, and led the
visitor only up dark staircases, through trap-doors,

into dungeons; and declining, also, to make the chief interest gather in some mailed knight who revelled and raided, he gave to the old manor-house the glad life of the true-hearted old gentleman, the well-mannered lady, the sport and kindnesses of old, not over-old, tradition. Perhaps he took up the thread which, in Sir Roger de Coverly, the essayist of the Spectator had commenced to weave. Whatever was the secret of his success, he was successful, and he deserved it. In his case, at least, the goddess Fortune of literature walked with unbandaged eyes and saw the right man and put him in the right place.

In 1841, a map, that was really very curious, came into my possession. It delineated the old possessions of the New Netherlands. It had vague ideas, indeed, of lakes and districts; and where now are the rich and prosperous lands of western New York, was on this a collection of hard, Indian designations, and quaint pictures of the savages' camps and wigwams. But, in one respect, it was rich and replete with information, and that was in the department of the Hudson river, where all the demands of the historian seemed to be met, in the blending of the aboriginal and the colonists' names of shore and mountain and village. I sent to Mr. Irving a copy of this map, and called his attention to the fact that over all the country on the border

14

of the river opposite his home, there was the record of thē ownership of the Heer Van Neder-horst. The name was new to me, as connected with manorial grant, but the map seemed to give him a domain so wide, that I considered it eminently worthy of research, to know who was this great " laird" of ten thousand Hudson river side acres.

His answer to my letter indicated that the gift of the map was to him a welcome one. He says : " I highly prize the historical document with which you have furnished me. When leisure presents, I will endeavor to study out this map with the lights afforded by old books and records, concerning the early history of the Hudson and its dependencies. My time and attention are, however, so much cut up and engrossed by a thousand domestic cares and concerns, that I seem daily to have less and less leisure and quietude for literary pursuits. I can only say, that the chords you have touched upon in your communications with me are such as are peculiarly in unison with my tastes and humors.

" As to the Heer Nederhorst, I have an idea that I have a memorandum concerning him among my papers, and that a Colonie or a Patroonship was granted to him on the west side of the river, on which he attempted to form a settlement, and to raise tobacco, but without success. I may be mistaken, but will look into the matter. I have been very desirous of ferreting out the original Indian names. Many of them are contained in the old title-deeds, and may be found in the clerk's offices of the various river counties. I have rescued two or three localities in my own neighborhood from their vile, commonplace names, and restored to them their wild Indian names, which happened to be quite euphonious."

Some years afterward, the Senate of the State of New York, on the motion of the Hon. George R. Babcock, of Buffalo, directed its clerk to procure the " restoration " of an old portrait, declared to be of Columbus, which in a long, long time past, had been presented to the Senate by Maria Farmer, a descendant of Jacob Leisler. It seemed to the clerk, as he examined the history of the gift, that its descent from Leisler was a very curious and interesting feature. That unfortunate, but distinguished man had been the martyr to his adherence to the Revolution of 1688, — to his faith in the more liberal principles for which William of Orange had come to the sovereignty of England. He had travelled in Europe, and it seemed most probable that he had brought this portrait home with him, as purporting to be of a name everywhere the property of America. The picture was admirably restored by Williams, Ste-

vens, and Williams, and it is at this hour an ornament of the senate chamber.

The clerk of the Senate wrote a report of his
fulfilment of his duty, which, on the motion of the
Hon. John A. Cross, of Brooklyn, was entered
on the journals of the Senate, and a copy of this
volume of the journals was directed to be sent to
Mr. Irving, which was done, and this grateful
acknowledgment made: —

> " SUNNYSIDE, February 23, 1851.
> " DEAR SIR, — I have the honor to acknowledge the re-
> ceipt of your letter of the 27th January, accompanying
> copies of a resolution of the Senate, and of its Journal for
> the session of 1850. On referring to the appendix to that
> journal, I am made sensible of the signal compliment in-
> tended me by the Senate in directing the transmission of
> this document.
> " To be deemed by that honorable and enlightened body,
> worthy to have my name in any degree associated with that
> of the illustrious discoverer, whose achievements I have at-
> tempted to relate, is, indeed, a reward beyond the ordinary
> lot of authors.
> " I am unacquainted with the forms of the Senate, but I
> beg you will communicate in a suitable way to that honora-
> ble body, my deep and grateful sense of this very flattering
> mark of their consideration."

I doubt if Mr. Irving ever realized thoroughly
the full measure of popularity which he really possessed with the people, making his name one of the

few in the value of which all men united, and of which the nation was earnestly proud.

·   In 1857, I visited him at Sunnyside, making a delightful preface to such a visit, by an hour at the house of his neighbor and intimate friend and kinsman, the Hon. M. H. Grinnell.   In all respects, — in the society that accompanied me, — in the day, — in the preliminary ride through Wolfert's Dell, with its beautiful landscape, such a picture of beauty hanging over the Hudson, — in all these, it was a visit that was to me a memorable one.   Sunnyside, as long as stone and lime shall bind together, will be attractive in association.   It deserves attraction from its own tasteful and cosey appointments, — being, in plan and form and in situation, much nearer the solid of an ideal, than it is often given to genius to achieve.

Soon after we arrived at the house, Mr. Irving came in, and his way and manner impressed me as being very active and lively, not at all over-mannered, but with a joyous friendliness, that was very agreeable to the visitor.   His conversation was delightful, anecdotical, continuous, and full of enjoyment.   He eulogized Moore and rejoiced in Scott, — especially exulting in the memory of the days he passed at Abbottsford, and his manner of uttering this was very impressive.   "I said to myself," said he, "in the evening of each of those days, this has been a perfectly happy day. Now mind — I said it then — I do not say it now." I understood this to mean that he conveyed to me his conviction that it was not through the pleasant maze of colored memories that he expressed his enjoyment, but that he had said this eulogy of the days, while they were with him, and while all detail, all incident, was vivid in his recollection.

An allusion was made to the delight with which a young lady who was with me had read his Tales of Alhambra. Instantly he started up with great animation, and walking rapidly across the room, said, "Oh, I can show her a portion of the frieze of one of its walls," — which he did. I remember his defending Moore against the charge, which his autobiographical diary would seem to prove, that he isolated himself in his social pleasures, without his wife's participation, even when they were the gayeties of the neighborhood, — as in the instance of his many delightful visits to Lord Lansdowne's mansion, Bowood, — Mr. Irving said that Mrs. Moore declined to accompany him. She saw or believed she saw that there was a distinction in the welcome to, or in the position of, the great author and his wife, and hence, in what we should call "standing on her dignity," she remained at home. In a letter subsequent to that visit, Mr. Irving alluded to Moore's writing concerning this country : —

"Moore was a very young man when he visited this country, and lived to regret the wrong impressions he received and published concerning its inhabitants. I wonder Lord John Russell, who was his literary executor, did not omit some insulting passages contained in those early letters, which I am convinced, Moore himself would have obliterated, had he revised them for the press."

These hours at Sunnyside, — seeing Mr. Irving surrounded by the kindred to whose happiness his life seemed one constant devotion —with the audit of his genial talk — himself in full life and good spirits — his themes the great minds with whom he had held more intimate association than had any other man in America, — these were hours that it would be treason to one's own highest enjoyment to forget. As we left, he accompanied us to the outer door, and passing a little room, said in his terse, emphasized way : " There — there is the place where I am busy at my work (the Life of Washington) — busy at it — putting the dead coloring on."

It was the " dead coloring " in the progress of the intellectual picture then, but history has framed it in her gallery of portraits; that will abide the look of the ages.

I saw him afterward at church, at Tarrytown, and of all persons I think he was the most attentive. It must have been in him the high good manners of principle, for I do recollect that the sermon was especially cold and uninteresting. He seemed to me different from his portraits,— so much so, that when he entered the room at Sunnyside, it was a surprise to me. I have since stood by Palmer's side, as he, from photograph and sketch, was moulding the bust which is such a triumph of his art, and I thought in that I could see Mr. Irving as he looked in life. There was a turn of his features toward the utterance of, or relish for, a pleasantry, a quick discernment of the ludicrous, and in his face the expression of a man with a solidity of comfort about him. Eliot, the great portrait painter, told me that when he (Mr. Eliot) went up to Sunnyside specially to make semblance of him, Mr. Irving laughingly declined. " No," said he, " I shall not perpetuate such a libel on myself as to have a picture of an old man made, and then to hear it said, ' Is this the old fellow who has written all those tender love stories?' Oh, no, that wont do!"

CHAPTER VI.

ONFINED, almost without exception, as these records are, to the memories of those who have left the land of the living, and fully defined history and character, I hoped not to have included the name of Edward Everett. I even thought that, perhaps, he might give this book the honor of a perusal for he had so kindly noticed, in a specific chapter of his Mount Vernon papers, a former work, the Life of Daniel Boone, written by me.

But the inexorable fate of all overtook him, and he died in the strength of his fame, without twilight to his long day of service to mankind and of honor to himself. No apologies for decadence dimmèd that fame. He died while a nation was gazing at him, and the universal grief of the nation was the wail at his grave. He had been the utterer of the oracles of holy writ, and the traditions of that time were a precious memory, a legend of gold and frankincense and myrrh, brought to

(217)

the holy treasury ; he had taken the uppermost place among American scholars, and gave to that name a solid and a sure worth, which made it recognized in the old world of intense student and tested learning; he had, in his department of oratory, risen where he was not even. rivalled ; of statesmanship, of diplomacy, he had had and held the best and worthiest; he was illustrious to his very townsmen ; and thus he died in his seat on the dais of his race, and the head of the nation led the nation to mourn over him. His ambition could have compassed in its imaginings no worthier name or fame.

He had seen all the wisest and the worthiest. The welcomed guest of Scott, acquaintance of Byron, and these typing all the long list of excellences and dignities,— having seen all these closely and intimately, knowing the best of the past and great in the present, what was there more that was " of the earth, earthy " for his illustration or experience ?

I first saw Edward Everett, if I may say I saw him, in the twilight, and its shades deeper than its light, of a September evening, on the Common, at Boston, in 1851, beneath a great tent, or pavilion, which had been spread over a large space there, in which to give a banquet to the guests at Boston's most hospitable Railway Jubilee. That city believed itself bound to the Canadas, and indeed to

all mankind, by the chain of iron it had forged by
its enterprise; and this was the coming together
of the wisest and the worthiest to felicitate state
and nation, and especially each other, that so
much was well and worthily done. Mr. Everett
was about fifty-six years of age, certainly in his
prime, although his whole life was in great degree
worthy of being styled thus. It had been a day
of great festivity. The pageant had almost exhausted Boston's decorative skill. The procession
had innumerable devices, and very curious and
very beautiful they were. The schools were there,
and there•was the charm. There were artificers
in all•the precious stones in the display, but there
were the workers in mind, "more precious than
rubies." ˗ The true treasures of the city were
there, and they told where its strength lay; and if
Canadians conned that lesson well, their visit had
something better than the memories of a gala day.
The boys were orderly,— that was eulogy enough.
In the thronging crowd, room was made for the
girls to walk through safely. Men unused to parlor life did this kindly; and this true chivalry,
exercised toward the gentle and defenceless, won
my admiration more than would a myriad of the
·studied and often interested courtesies of men
toward each other,— the practising with a masque,
as so much of it is. There was a miniature Ætna

in the line; it smoked sneezingly. I doubt if the
mountain is as odoriferous. There was a fire-
worker, who had a wizard before, and a great vam-
pyre bat in the rear of his vehicle, puzzling everybody, and acting with a dramatic excellence that
would have won a smile from Garrick.

I remember with what genius for contrast the
pianoforte-makers made their display. An old box
of 1793, looking up from its cracked jingle to a
gorgeous grand, all-radiant, in rosewood, and with
a tone that would touch the music nerve even of
that musicless man that Shakspeare anathematizes.

Through all this labyrinth of dainty and rare
devices, the three thousand guests of Boston
wended their way to the pavilion; and although
the vast army of spectators were subjected to the
most severe ordeal of submission that can occur to
man, — seeing others going to dinner when they
are not,— yet there was the grandeur of a quiet
adherence to all the arrangements of the day. It
was a proud day for the good order of Boston.
Generally, the people that go to these great public
feasts, like those who are found at the elegant sup-
pers of fashion, are of a class of people who live at
home very well, certainly with quite enough and in
abundance of the aliment of life. Why is it, then,
that such people generally eat with such vigor and
with such persevering relish? Evidently the

causes lie deep within. We drank the coffee, and
did not murmur for champagne; and in the aroma
of the Arabian berry there was abundant merri-
ment.

The President of the United States (Mr. Fill-
more) was a guest, and at his side was the Governor of the Canadas (Elgin and Kincardine);
and when, in the opening speech, these representative men grasped each other's hands, it was dramatic. We all felt the beauty of the incident, and
the great crowd in the pavilion was stirred with
feeling, as witnessing something more than a personal courtesy. Lord Elgin made a very good
speech, — effective, bright, right on, with American facility of utterance. I had seen him before,
acting as the representative of the Crown, in the
Parliament, at Toronto, upon the Council throne,
the Council before him, the Commons at the bar;
Lord Frederick Bruce, since prominent in China,
at his side, and himself buttoned cruelly close in
blue and silver. We all thought him a man of
eloquent expression, educated language, and clear
good sense; and when Victoria's health was given,
the pavilion thousands sent forth a cheer that
calmed the old echoes that might have haunted
these revolutionary streets. Then might a smile
have come to the lip of the dead of the Old Province House. It was one of the hours of that

which Mr. Monroe called, "the era of good feeling."

Long before the audience wanted to leave, the darkness of the evening closed around us, and the eloquent voices came to us out of the obscure; and strange and quaint it was to catch the different lights and shadows of this great crowd, all listening in attention, while but few could with any distinctness see the speakers.

I there first heard the voice of Edward Everett, and the chord of the master-hand was revealed. That sweet and strong enunçiation, those sculptured sentences, that wealth of imagery, the pleasant and fitting illustrations, — all these went to the heart of the audience and made his address the favorite of the occasion.

This magnificent banquet — so in its intellectual food, though simple in that which ministered to the mortal part — closed. All that remained for the jubilee was to light up park and hall and mansion, with brilliant illumination, and this was charmingly done. I stood by the crescent sheet that the Cochituate spreads on the common. In the beautiful light of the day, the fountain, springing from its long journey of aqueduct and tube, seemed glistening in joy at its release. It formed its arch of crystal, breaking, dissolving, — now a silver sheet and now a feathery plume. This

night, the rocket and the Bengola light flung their
vivid green and red and white brilliancy toward
the sky, and this pure spring-water formed a mirror for all the beauty of the gay fires above, and
the ripples turned to emerald or azure or crimson
as each arched over it. Except as these bars of
light existed for the moment, the Common was
densely dark and gloomy in its foliage. From the
ancient cemetery of Copp's Hill, from all the
avenues, the fires went up, and giant torches
seemed quivering over Boston.

I remember that old John Hancock's house, from
the ancient attic to the parlors, — not less curious
and old-fashioned, — was in full illumination.
Amidst this labyrinth of light and shadow this
jubilee ended ; and it was a pleasant thought to
associate one's first knowledge of such a name as
that of Everett with so much of beauty.

In 1853, the people of Plymouth called to that
ancient town — that town so buried up under a
cairn of eulogies, of odes, of speeches, of all
that something of history and much of imagination
can effect, — all who desired to breathe the air
of the ocean in the fervid month of August ; all
who desired to know the capabilities of Plymouth
for a gala day ; and all who wished to hear Edward
Everett utter his noble words of philosophical
beauty in and around the Rock. Of the 22d of

December, as memorialized at this town, we had often heard; but the wild coast winds and driving snows were no incentive to hospitality, and so our ingenious friends contrived this celebration of the Embarkation of the Pilgrims, or, as one of the legends in the street, wittily called it — Forefather's Day thawed out. Of course, thither we moved, having Mrs. Hemans' stanzas as our text of thought, and looking closely out for that " stern and rock-bound shore." I recollect that being compelled, by some miscalculation of railway hour, to take the long drive from Centre Abington, we doubted in the midnight if there was such place as Plymouth, — whether it was not all a myth, and Elder Brewster and the Rock and the Mayflower were not shadowy as Homer's heroes and battle-fields. But the horses were good and the driver was sober. We read guide-boards by cigar-light, and the Samoset at last by its watch said to us, Welcome, Englishmen ; or, if not thus literally following the Indian's unexpected, voice, gave us that which Shenstone declares a real pleasure — the welcome of an inn. It puzzled us how the wearied May-flower found its way thither. The town was in situation and circumstance very different from the thought yesterday cherished in respect to it. The current idea of it is of a small and very old settle-ment, with a bold, bluff point projecting out into

the sea; and the Rock, the most auspicious feature of the scene. Such is the Plymouth of the
mind; but the reality is different. Behind two or
three enfoldings of cape and beach and sea-wall, it
is about the last place into which a vessel would be
sure to come as a matter of course. It must have
perplexed the solemn sailors to have found their
way inward. It is a shelter from the sea. One
hears the moaning of the ocean, but it is heard as
we hear the rain on the roof.

But where is the Rock? Right out in the open
sea, we thought, — its bold, age-worn surface swept
by every storm. So we rushed to find it, — if, indeed, we were not rather disappointed that it was
not seen far above all edifices, the great landmark
of the coast. Not first to have gone to it, would
have been to neglect St. Peter's on a visit to Rome.
We found Mrs. Hemans and the romance of history poor guides; so threading our way through
narrow streets, with " ancient and fish-like " pecu-
liarities, with stores bearing the old sign of West
India goods, around corners and through lanes,
we traced it out at last, — some benevolent individual having written its locality, for the use and
behoof of strangers, not in letters of granite or
iron, but in a chalk formation; and at last we stood
upon the Rock, — that is, on so much of it as the
debris and neglect and shocking bad taste and
15

historical neglect of this people had left above-
ground.   Was this our Mecca?   I could absolve
myself and reflect that westward lineage of my own
had smoked peaceable pipes on Castle Island many
years before this world-moving expedition reached
Plymouth.   We returned to the Samoset, wiser
and sadder.   We afterward found high and dry
in the main street, encompassed with a railing, a
great piece of the Rock, reft from its historical
place; and we recollected that a fragment of it
does duty as a curiosity in a Brooklyn steeple.
But we sorrowed in all good earnest over the
fatality that seems to attach in our country to all
historical monuments.

Pleasanter associations soon effaced this.   Old
Plymouth seemed set in a crown of flowers, and
wherever we looked some of those fair girls, — who
keep up the lineage of handsome Penelope Pel-
ham, whose portrait, in Pilgrim Hall, fascinated
us, — everywhere these had adorned arch and
roof and corridor and balcony with floral loveli-
ness, and we were at once fascinated followers in
the train of the daughters of the May and August
flower.

The morning brought with it a fog, the afternoon a sweet sunshine, and thus the Pilgrim's
experiences were symboled.   The heavens often
write such lessons in their shining and their

shadows. I saw in the gathering to the Tent, a procession of ladies, and they moved on in a most orderly way, perhaps because of the grand review of look and observation which was before them. The scene in the Pavilion was a beautiful one; for it was a gathering of such order, such respectability, and in that crowd of fair women, so much of beauty; and it is pleasant to chronicle, that was the day when the fashion of the bonnet was of the very prettiest. Up on the dais came Gov. Clifford, and the elder Quincy, and Hale, Sumner, and, as the master mind of all — Everett. It was a circle of illustrious names, and they had before them an appreciative audience.

At that time, one of the leading themes that was woven into all public address and private conversation, was the subject of the extension of our territorial area, — a little restlessness toward Cuba and Central America. The tiger had tasted Texas. It was also a day when the absurdity of the spiritual rappings was in its height or its depth. Mr. Everett was superb. His audience hushed at the sound of his magnificent sentences.

Has Plymouth ever really raised the monument, of which this was to be the hour of origin? If it has not, then is there a great duty left undone, and we shall be free to believe her ardent sons rather insincere in their adulation. A few old houses to come

down, an area of old wharf to be demolished, and
it seemed as if the Rock might again be bound to
the sea,— fit base for some lofty pile of commemo-
ration.   I think if New York could identify the
exact spot where Hendrick Hudson first landed on
the Island of Manhattan, our Historical Society
would never rest till granite made its memory permanent.   *   *

   I remember that there was a model there of the
Mayflower, — a tall, high-decked, clumsy affair.
It is not wonderful that the dear old ship made a
four months' voyage: Scant form of the clipper
is there about her, and in a race to California, the
Flying Cloud could give her start as far as Cape
Horn, and then reach the Golden Gate and begin
to discharge cargo before she arrived.   Scott, in
his Peveril of the Peak, says that England cast
forth the Pilgrims as a drunkard loses from his lap
precious jewels.

   It was a day of good memories.   I would have
thought it a little more in the gratitude of true
history, had I seen, amidst the profusion of bunt-
ing that floated everywhere, the flag of Holland,
which had for so many months sheltered the Pilgrims, and whose large and lofty hospitality made
that land of the sea the refuge for the free thought
of all countries.

   At night, Plymouth was bright with festal fires,

and glad in the harmonies of skilled music. Rock-
ets, bursting into stars of polychrome, made radiant
messengers so far in the upper air, that it may be
distant vessels, on their ocean way, made note in
their nautical record of strange meteors playing in
the heavens in the latitude of the Rock, and weird
legends might have been thus woven of celestial
colors, making memorial of the Pilgrims' varied
fortunes.

At a very agreeable "reception," given in the
evening of that memorable day, I think at the
house of Mr. Warren, in the course of the conversation, I mentioned to Mr. Everett, that when a
student in the law-office of the distinguished Harmanus Bleecker, of Albany, whom I knew to be a
great favorite with the Boston people, with Mr.
Appleton and the Quincys, and with Mr. Everett
himself, Mr. Bleecker, as a choice morsel amidst
the dry hard tack of the law, had allowed me to
read, in manuscript, a sermon of Mr. Everett's
delivery, when clergyman of a church in Boston;
and that I could well recollect my delight in it.
It was upon the text, "Who will show us any
good?"

In the description of this festival, reference
was made to sentences in his address which
seemed to me to take a surprisingly mild view
of the then advancing idea of the filibuster,

as the disturbers of the peace of nations were called. — Under date of August 12, 1853, he very kindly alludes to this narrative of the Plymouth celebration, and says: " I think if you will carefully read my remarks, you will not find them open to the exception intimated by yourself. I spoke only of the transfer of the culture of the Old World (with the requisite improvements) to the New. To meet exceptions which had been taken, in several cases invidiously, to the same sentiment expressed by me on former occasions, I took care, by three or four qualifying clauses, to exclude the inference that this was necessarily to be done under any one political organization. You will ask, perhaps, why use at all a language so likely to be misunderstood and confounded with the doctrine of the filibusters? To this question there are two answers. . First, it is impossible to say anything warmly and earnestly which will not be both misapprehended and misrepresented. Second, I use such language for much the same reason that led Wesley to set his hymns to good music. I wish to show the country that a sound and true conservatism does not require one to be eternally croaking, and is not insensible to the hopes and glories of that future to which the analogy of the past authorizes us to look forward."

He then requests me to aid him in procuring for

him the sermon to which I have alluded. " I have been for years endeavoring to obtain the return of my manuscripts of every kind, that I may, while I live, make such selection and disposition of them as may save trouble to those who come after me."

It was my great good fortune to be present at the festival of the United States Scientific Association, held at Albany, in August, 1856. I doubt whether any *fête* more successful was ever known in our country, in the character of those who gathered and in the high tone of talent which distinguished all that was said or done, and of all which the address, on the uses of Astronomy, by Mr. Everett, was far away the master-piece, the intellectual crown.

I remember that Albany was a very busy place at that time ;. for besides the convention of savans, there was a gathering of those who studied in political convention the laws of power. There was a welcome given to the savans at the capitol. The great rooms of that edifice were appropriate, in their diversity and magnitude, for all the purposes of hospitality. The Assembly and Senate halls received learned gentlemen and lovely ladies ; and those who had seen the capitol in so many other uses, confessed its rare fitness to enable us to realize what must be the capacities of the castle structures of Europe to the services of opulent entertainment. The fullest flounce of fashion had room and verge enough. Once before that capitol opened its doors to festive uses. It was when Lafayette, as the Guest of the Nation, was received there, and when a ballroom was found — a superb one indeed — in the Assembly chamber.

The successive sessions, during the week, of the different sections of the meeting left the visitor in embarrassment, in the copious treasure of mental power everywhere offered to him. It was the American scholar urged to indicate his best by the presence of his peers, and there were offerings on the altar of science where abiding good might safely be predicted. It was the evidence of the great advance of our people out of the struggling life of frontier pioneer poverty to the riches of intellectual excellence; and as if to bind all this to the past, I´ saw there one who stood by the side of Governor Clinton as the first earth was moved for the construction of the canal,— one who was fellow-passenger with Robert Fulton in the first voyage by steam.

It was very interesting to observe the scholars of America,— the scholars in science,— for our possession of a great array of such is often doubted and probably wisely doubted, by ourselves. We do not do for mental treasure what we do for the oil,— dig long and deep and unceasingly, through all obsta-

cle, over all difficulty. In no country, as much.
as in ours, does patience *not* perform its entire
work. We crowd life with the desperate effort to
know something of all things. Perhaps this *is*
wise, the greatest wisdom. It is a question not
settled yet. Some of these savans were thorough, and had their one department of science :
thus, Henry R. Schoolcraft was patient in his investigation into the ethnology of the Indian. Perhaps I was impressed with the seeming glamour of
his ideas about their language, their words those
of necessity. They lived an existence of alarm
amidst the gloom of the wood, and did not disturb
the Faun and Satyr by over-much intrusion of
sound into the forest shadow. Not till civilization
came did they make record of their tongue. The
language of labor was English ; the language of
their diplomacy, their inter-governmental commu-
nication as of themselves, the Algonquin.

An intelligent captain of a merchant vessel gave
graphic illustration of the benefit he had derived
from his belief in Mr. Redfield's law of storms.
The circle is the path of the storm ; and the rules
of the savan enabled the sailor to exercise a watch-
fulness which seemed like reading the future.
This captain's vessel was proceeding from Valpa-
raiso to New York, and he and all his crew desired ,
to make it, if possible, of all voyages, the speediest ;

and thus pressed on by the full-aired canvas, the ship went at a rate of progress that promised a speedy look at the lights of home. The captain observed facts which he believed were exponents, according to Mr. Redfield, of proximate danger. His authority was supreme; but when he gave the order to shorten sail and delay, all on board thought it a foolish sacrifice to the illusion of a theory. But his was a ship where obedience followed command, and the ship paused, paused as it eventuated on the edge of the circle of destruction; for, when he resumed his course, and at last reached Sandy Hook, the pilots had but one color of tidings to communicate, and that was of the darkest, for a more wild and fearful storm had scarcely ever poured out its might; and but for that delay, influenced by that theory, the ship would have met that storm in all its power.

I heard much of geological discussion. It was the very place to hear it in its best array of ingenious theory and puzzling fact. An eminent geologist (Mr. James Hall) presided over the great assemblage of savans. These wise men wandered into regions of fore-time. They traced out, in the strata, the slowly accumulating developments of life; they bewildered us by their profound and elaborate doctrines; and we who could not controvert, and were too polite to contradict, heard, and were as amazed as they could have desired. But, at this comfortable distance, I must say, even if the saying depresses my volume, that it seems to me that there is not a geological appearance, or a zoological indication, however buried up or concealed or blended with rock, or immersed in drift, on hill-top or under ocean bed, but that every difficulty fades before the great explanation of the Deluge. An earth created with all the unities of formation, has poured upon it the terrific forces of an all-pervading overflow. The fountains of the great deep break up. Over all the terrific ocean rises with a dread so awful, that only then in the history of Time is such power permitted. The promise is painted in the heavens that never again shall such be. Then the Earth rises from its encounter with such forces a different structure; torn, crushed, displaced, there is everywhere change, modification, transformation. While the summit of Ararat was under the wave, the work of ages was accomplished.

The section appropriated to the Astronomers was very abstruse, but the ladies were special visitants to the star-gazers. It was a contemptible servility; but it was a curious word used by the old poet Rogers, uttered to one of our own citizens, when talking with him about death, — "I want to go, Mr. ——," said he, "when I die, from star to star, to see in which of them woman is found."

These men of the ethereal study uttered learn-
* ing at which the common mind quails. I was
drowned in the depths of the discourse upon the
tidal currents of Saturn's Ring. The address was
doubtless worthy, for it received the high honor of
Joseph Henry's attention. If but the man who
was in Albany one hundred and two years before
this date (Franklin), could have been at this gathering, he would have seen the development of the
road to which his sparkling kite-string led. The
enlightenment given by one savan, of the nebular
hypothesis, was beyond ordinary comment. When
Science undertakes to dance redowas and schot-
tisches and mazourkas, those of us who, in ordinary affairs, might take partners, are content to be
amazed.

Charles Lamb wrote upon a leaf of his book of
calculation, which lay on his desk at the India
House, " *This increases in interest as you progress.*"
It was so of the days of this Scientific Congress,
and its narrative has detained me from the special
theme of this chapter — Mr. Everett. I saw him
presented to the body, whose institution of the
Observatory had called the Congress of Savans
together, and he next appeared on the stage at the
closing day of the Association, the day just previous to the Inauguration of the Dudley Observatory. This closing day was brilliant with Agassiz

and Bache and Sir William Logan and Joseph
Henry and President Anderson, all of whom, as I
write, are living, and fulfilling the high promise of
their talent. I like to watch a crowd while a man
of intellect utters forth the strength of his thought.
The ladies listen with such unfeigned attention,
trusting and believing, and the men half suspect-
ing, half yielding to the fascination.

The venerable and very bright Dr. Samuel H.
Cox amused us all by a clever episode. He said
he had been talking, when in Europe, with a distinguished titular personage, who said the United
States were but the *selvage* of society. "No
wonder," said the Doctor to him, "that you forget
us,—we often forget you; we are a continent,—
you are but an island. If you will come over to
us in the form of an island, we will find you a lake
big enough to swim in!"

This Congress was a very popular one. The
community have a mysterious respect for men who
know so much. It is an enlarged and enlightened
descent from the feeling of the darker ages, when
the learned clerks moved gloomily from shrine to
shrine.

The Inauguration Day had its clouds, and one
savan who had promulgated his theory of storms,
was assailed by questioning as to what was indicated by them; and he answered us with a degree

of confidence which reminded me of the weather predictions of Norna of the Fitful Head.

In the front of the dais sat Everett, Agassiz, Silliman, and none would dispute their right to be in that roll of honor. After delays and interlocutory proceedings, all clever in their own way and time, but painfully protracting the coming of the event for which that crowd had gathered, — the discourse of Edward Everett, — he rose. I knew his address was all thoroughly prepared. Indeed, it was already in type. I had it in my possession already; he had given it to me on the previous evening, at the hospitable reception at the Manor House. He knew that I would not betray him by premature publication. I have since known that he passed several hours of the day on which he pronounced the discourse in *intense* study, so intense that it left its severe impress on his physical condition.

Of the grandeur of that discourse this testimony need not be given. It to-day is read by all men who seek the beauty of their own language. Without looking at note or brief, his gigantic memory unrolled his long address,— not a word misplaced, without confusion or entanglement or error. I was perpetually interrupted in my interest at its glowing charm of expression, its most felicitous figure, so thoroughly sustained to the absorbing climax, by my amazement at his memory. It was precise. In describing the bridges over the Arno, in his picture of Florence, he intended to say that they hovered over, rather than spanned, the river, and he half used the word span first, and before the word was all pronounced, recovered himself; so intensely true was his memory to him. He moved in a constant but gentle walk over a space of ten feet ; his gestures natural, unless the tremor of his hand was an art ; his utterance very distinct, but his voice that day not doing justice to its sweetness, being veiled in the difficulties of a sad cold.

Over and again this Astronomical Discourse may be read. I bear record that it was heard with intense interest, and to all that vast audience this was a grandeur of oratory. When it closed, I left the ground with a gentleman not at all favorably disposed toward Mr. Everett. Keen, cold, acute in his criticism, a very able and a very prominent man, master of his own thought, and controlling the public mind in great degree. " *He has conquered me*," said he to me. I knew how much was meant by this testimony. I recollect Mr. William Logan, the eminent geologist of the Canadas, said, " I did not think the English language capable of this." The long and fully kept up passage in which he described the successive glories of the starry night's pathway to the sunrise, thrilled that crowd. I *know* that this was the emotion of that hour, and it seems to me well to chronicle .thus what were the exact lineaments of a time so memorable as that of the delivery of one of the great addresses of the age, by the orator who, in his department, was unrivalled.

There were many clergymen, and distinguished ones, in attendance. I would like to have gathered there all the synods, conventions, assemblies, conferences, convocations, and consociations, and for this one purpose, that they might have seen and heard how much men gain in their addresses to the human heart by speaking them, not reading,— by the utterance of voice, sustained by manner and gesture and eye.

When Mr. Everett commenced — suffering as he did from a cold — I feared for his success. I had heard him in the strength of health and fairest tone of voice; but I bear his fame witness, he was all•himself. He spoke with such beauty, that I hesitate now to say whether I ever admired his witchery of speech more than on this occasion. Such sentences, so much of elaborate preparation, and yet carried from memory into voice so successfully!

I watched this cold man — for so many called him — to see if emotion was kindled in him of his own thought. I saw his cheek flush and his eye kindle, and found no chill of the wheel of life there.

The darkness of the evening shadowed the tent before this memorable Festival of Eloquence was over. It was a proud historic day for Albany, and some monumental record of that gathering should be placed where it was held.

There is, in the series of Mr. Everett's Mount Vernon papers, a chapter in which he alludes to his experiences of the sleeping-car, then just introduced, and one of the great onward movements toward comfort in travelling. When Young uttered that famous expression, " We take no note of time save by its loss," he did not know the gentlemen of the railway. The conductor keeps his finger on the pulse of the old graybeard, and values every throb. I have often thought that no cause in our American experience has done so much to teach Americans the value of every minute of time, as has the railway system. 6.17 means something very practical when one arrives at a station at 6.20, and finds in these fractions, hitherto disregarded, the labor of his morning lost. Whoever has, for his sins, been compelled to travel at night before the sleeping-car was prepared, knows that the time is occupied in varying one's position so as to arrive at the exact weight of the head, and what degree of the tortuous and the twisted the vertebræ of the neck will bear. Contrast this with the luxury of an outstretched limb,

16

a space and circumstance of rest if not of sleep,—
something of quiet; the roar of the wheel beneath
at last blending into a dream,—a thought confusing
itself into the sweet chaos of welcome sleep. Not
possessing a talent for sleep, I have often heard the
wheel till my ear seemed at the engine's heart, listening to its pulsation. The locomotive carries us
on its giant arms, and the eye that closes in the
shadowy pictures of the Mohawk, awakes amidst
the life of Rochester. Mr. Everett complained of
being interrupted in his sleep by conversation 'between two railway officials. It is seldom that

> "The censer of censure is swung,
>   And returns with the incense of praise."

I assured him that there was not an officer of the
road, from president to brakesman, who would not
willingly sit up all night, even after a day of labor,
to listen to his utterances of words in beauty.
Indeed, the best compliment, because fresh and
original, of all I ever heard given to Mr. Everett,
was by a railway man. We were all at Bing-
hampton, listening to Mr. Everett's glorious discourse on Washington. The admission fee was
fifty cents. When the address finished, this man
turned from his wrapt attention to his friend who
sat next him, and says he, " *This ought to have
been a dollar !* "

This oration impressed me not only as a great

tribute to the labors of the Scientific Association, but more than that, as a mastery. Our minds all the week had been at the feet of the philosophy, which, great as it is, is but the discovery of the greater or the better in the things that are seen. Here rose this man, in melody of voice and glory of thought, above all the theories of strata and classification, which were yesterday unknown, to-day are doubted, and to-morrow will be overthrown. How swept his voice over the chords of the human heart! We live but in the Present, and the great Orator is master of the Present. To him Science is not the messenger; it does but bring the marble out of which *he* carves the glorious statue.

It *was* something to be a witness of the scenes of that day when Boston, by an address from Edward Everett, inaugurated the bronze statue of Daniel Webster; for how could more suitable orator find more felicitous theme? A civilized human race seeks to perpetuate the remembrance of the men who have risen, by good or great deed, above their fellow-beings. It is the symbolizing of Memory, and by the consent of the ages, the statue is most appropriate. It has the material over which the fingers of the years pass softly. Europe has its halls and galleries and arches crowded with such forms of resemblance. All that the heart could desire in the beauty and truth of resemblance of those that the heart holds dearest, the sculptor makes in perpetual form. Old Rome did not forget to teach the earth this lesson, in company with those by which the dead Lion yet governs the mind of mankind.

These graven memorials Boston is accumulating, and the treasure cannot be too great. Washington, Franklin, Warren, Bowditch, Story, in marble and in bronze, are there. Even the sweet stranger, Beethoven, is there, and the group would have been incomplete without the statue of Webster!

When I eulogize statuary as the most fitting memorial of men, I must, in my sense of truth, say, that the bronze statue is, of all others, least agreeable. Its color is not a truth. Perhaps I should be answered, that the fair white Carrara would be equally as unfaithful to the swart complexion of the great Constitutional Statesman; yet it is the pleasantest delusion at least. Of course, bronze is the only material-that can abide our climate; yet our great cities possess halls and other sheltering places, where the fatal frost and severe sun could not write their lines of change and decay, and the hall could be built for the statue, since, in its association, it would most commend itself to the popular favor.

The day opened,— so did not the clouds; yet a darker shadow than this preceded the day, that memorable day, when Webster crowned ·Bunker Hill Monument. One need not wonder at the myriad of statues that are found in Athens and in Rome. Whenever an inauguration day was needed for them, a delicious sky looked down in soft approval, while Grecian girls and Roman ladies looked up with delight. We have faint promise of any such carnival of weather when our holidays of public gathering come. The New York State Agricultural Fair has been the occasion of an elaborate study of meteorology.

This was a famous historical day in Boston. The " settlement " of Boston was two hundred and twenty-nine years old. Very absurd it was in the people of this peninsula, on the 17th day of September, 1630, to vote away from themselves the Indian-born designation of Shawmut, and in its place to bestow on themselves, on their picturesque peninsular home, the copy of an English village, itself bearing the name, decayed and dusted, from that of old Saint Botolph. But what right has any man of a state or city which obliterated its first nomenclature before the alternate titles of the Duke of York, to make this criticism? Remembering Man-hat-ta, silence best becomes "the occasion."

The bells rang out this morning from steeples that have shaken with peals proclaiming peace or announcing victory. The voice of the cannon spoke out the birthday of the city. I found, in the midst of the pouring rain, a positive pleasure in witnessing what beauty of arrangement the city had made.

The preparations for this celebration had been elaborate. With the English idea of thoroughness, which Boston has inherited and preserved, the structures for the accommodation of the spectators are strongly built, so that a delightful period in an address shall not find for its reward a grand crash instead of a plaudit. The Bostonians have a special talent in celebrations. Being orderly, they arrange pageants and processions without danger of roughs or rowdies; being intelligent, they have read and remembered, and compile the affair with attention to effect; being educated, they understand when the festivals in the year, worthy of pageant, come round.

The entire area of the State House grounds was covered with a platform, of course immense in capacity, and with comfort of seat and protection of rail, and flowers well watered. In the centre was *the* STATUE, to the inauguration of which this day was to be devoted. The entire structure was surrounded with a drapery of green and purple, so that all the look of " shantyism " was lost. If but the sun of Italy had been the

sky-genius of the occasion! On my way thither,
I passed the statue of Franklin. The old man
bore the rain like a philosopher, as he was. Down
his bronze cheek and over his brazen nose fell the
drops; but he who sent a line to the electric cloud
was not to soften beneath the shower. Despite
the wet, a group of enthusiastic boys were explain-
ing to each other the scenes of his science and his
mechanics and statesmanship displayed on the pan-
elling of the pedestal. The statue of Washington was safe and dry in a crypt of the hall; and
thus we were spared the pain of witnessing the
undignified spectacle of a dripping Father of his
Country. I like that calm, cold crypt in which
Canova's work is placed, with the gravestone of
the English ancestral home of the Washingtons
before it. It is a refuge for one's quiet thought
and day-dream of Presidential dignity.

On this seacoast a north-east storm means something. In some other places, as by the shores of
the lakes fo Western New York, it is a power, a
bath, a sunshine smile; but the smiles are not seen
here. The cloudy curtain drew its fold thicker
and closer. Soldiers and citizens, societies and
associations, the strength and beauty of the city,
doubted the wisdom of walking through the rain.
Yet the preparations went on. Again the bells
rung and the cannon fired, and sexton and gunner

did · their duty in their voices of peace and war. It was an affair which could not be postponed. Fortunately, in a great city there are great roofings, and shelter is for the many as well as for the few ; and so the orders issued, that leaving behind the spacious and well-arranged platform, where the statue should stand in the midst of the multitude, - the audience should be gathered in the Music Hall.

Mr. Everett had anticipated this ; for, as the party most interested, he had probably acutely watched the weather ; and, as he had spoken such charming words of the skies and their starry architecture, he might be supposed to be their familiar. I had seen a note from him, in which he says, — " From present appearances, the exercises will have to be in the Music Hall, which, so far as I am concerned, I do not regret."

He knew that the open air is the most severe ordeal for oratory ; that to lose the voice in the horizonless circle before him, is to lose its command ; that the effort is to reach the greatest distance, and that the finer tones of the voice are injuriously affected by this. Our American orators have, in this, a very severe trial ; and it is a great tribute to their power, that they have so often succeeded. It has been their lot to talk to their fellow-men in field and forest, in all the wild accompaniment of the barbacue, and in the blended multitude of opposing parties; so that American eloquence has had all the education of Demosthenes by the raging sea-side.

The Legislature, in full attendance, in defiance of the storm, marched from the State House to the hall, with an escort of soldierly men, who feared no elemental strife, and to the sounds of music that cheered us in the gloom. On these law-makers of Massachusetts moved. Their gentlemen of the white rod kept all in place; and following them, as one walks safely near so much of power, I found access to the hall.

This Music Hall has ample dimension; and on platform and on floor and in galleries gave convenient place for hearing. At first the attendance was small, for the honorable legislators had arrived early; but we thus had time to look around, and see whoever of greatness should come among the audience,— such being the reward of the punctual. The galleries, appropriated to the ladies, were soon filled; showing the varied hues of ornament, which alike in saloon where it cannot rain, and in any country at the height of the wet season, the ladies *will* wear, having excellent reasons for such conduct, quite above the dull comprehension of man. In poured the solid and the fragile men of Boston, and the great hall soon showed that spectacle, always so impressive, of a vast crowd, a mighty concourse. They filled the building from floor to roof, and this, too, in a day when every consideration of comfort pointed to the inside of one's home.

The arrival of one man told the reason why that crowd was there. It was Edward Everett; and when he entered, the multitude realized that they were to be rewarded for all frowning of the gloomy sky. He had unusual difficulties before him in this oration, — not of the subject, for that was of the grandeur to which his mind came by step of nature,— but because the mind of all the country had thought it out and spoken it out. He had himself spoken of it repeatedly. But it was a theme involving discrimination and delineation of qualities existing beyond the hour. Mr. Webster's fame was of the blended statesman and philosopher, and needed the analysis of a master hand.

As soon as the rush of human beings had been calmed into order, a quarter door of lattice-work, at the rear of the platform, was thrown open, and then rolled forth the grand harmonies of the organ (not *the* organ which is now the glory of that hall), in its power swelling or soothing, as the score demanded. I have heard, when there were but very few present, the sweetness of the organ's note, as, with a master of the art at the keys, the hymn of the plaintive Pleyel was breathed softly and solemnly. It was, in contrast to this, to hear its strength over such a concourse.

And then a marshal, with a golden wand, brought the assemblage to due order, and prayer was made. A prayer is *never* a subject for criticism. A good prayer is neither long nor declarative; nor does it anticipate speech or sermon. The words of a prayer, we are wisely told, should be " few and well chosen."

Professor Felton, of Harvard, as the chairman of the committee under whose action the statue had been made, made the formal presentation to Mayor Lincoln. The Professor was interesting and classical, and spoke as a college-man should speak. His historical allusions were precise, and the more valuable because fully measured before uttered.

The Mayor and Governor Banks did admirably their duty in the order of the proceedings. Both are living, and out of the plan of this volume; and long, long delayed may be the duty of their biographer, who shall await that which is the only proper theme, a completed and concluded career.

Mr. Everett was not introduced, nor was there need of it. When he rose, such welcome was given him as would have taken the impediment from the tongue of Demosthenes. It was a welcome to be prized, for it was that of a vast throng

of educated and intelligent men; and what made
it of higher value, it was given him at his own
home.   He must have felt the worth of this,
deeply.   His address has passed into volume, and
is of that series of Public Discourses which form
Mr. Webster's proudest monument.   It has received the approbation of those who value, and
who know how to value, the words that are born
of intellect.   His voice was excellent, and it grew
clearer to the close.   Often hearing him, he
seemed to me, on this occasion, unusually earnest
in gesture, his delivery reaching, at times, the
fervid in character.   I had been anxious to hear
him at Boston, and amidst his associations of
friends, as I had in places remote and among strangers.   He proved himself here, as everywhere, the
same glowing, winning, charming orator.

Now, to me, the amazing feature of his address
was in this: I knew that he was not speaking *all*
that he had prepared, as he had shown me, in his
library, the day previous, the manuscript; and he
had, in relation to this, written a note, which is
before me, in which he says: " Being a good
deal too long to be spoken *in extenso*, I shall only
be able to speak parts of it to-day, in some portions
an abridgment.   This will give it rather a frag-
mentary and occasionally meagre appearance."

The circumstances of the day and the changed

programme caused him to add other portions appropriate to the hour.

Here was that wonderful memory, beyond all ordinary rule of tenacity, able not only to hold all, but to take up and let go, at pleasure, parts separate and removed from each other, destroying all reliance on continuity of connection or association, never resorting to note or memorandum, but faithful in all. Let any one who doubts the difficulty of this, try the task of placing in his memory a series of stanzas, and then to repeat them, omitting several at irregular intervals.

Some passages in this discourse were received with applause that was rapturous and resistless. When he used the nautical figure of Webster, as a ship-of-the-line going into battle, he touched the hearts of these dwellers by the sea,— those familiar with oakum and tar,— and I surmised one enthusiastic, bald-headed gentleman, who leaned frantically forward, to be a ship-captain, or the owner of a yacht, he seemed so to delight in the picture.

I never heard, in all oratory, anything more dramatic than Mr. Everett's recitation of the parable of the Pharisee and the Publican. It was wonderful, and I place it in my memory as the most impressive giving-forth of Scripture that I ever heard. In describing this afterward, I ventured to say, that he must forgive one of the most sincere of his ad-

mirers in doubting the exactness of propriety in
thus · using the Holy Word; as, while the *effect*
which he desired by the illustration was produced,
there seemed to be an oblique direction given to
the great thought.   Subsequently, he wrote to
me: " I did not intend, in my use of the parable of
the Pharisee and the Publican, to wander from the
intent in which it was spoken by the Great
Teacher; and I think I could show you that I
have not done so.   The intent of the parable is
not to teach that moral deficiency is a matter of
indifference, but that censure ought to come only
from the pure.   I have never known Mr. Webster
to be reviled by any man whom I supposed to be
better than himself."

The audience were evidently delighted with the
discourse.   Their attention was fixed and absorbing even amidst the reasoning and argumentative
portions, and to every climax or picture passage,
the enthusiastic voices rose in uncontrollable emotion.   I admired, but could not quite concede, his
desponding, but beautifully expressed, judgment,
of the fate of inventors, as instanced in the decision of the Supreme Court of the United States
against Robert Fulton, when he claimed the exclusive right to navigate, by use of steam, the Hudson.   No; though Fulton was poor, and John
Fitch died a maniac, other and brighter pages are

read by invention in this age of clearer view and truer judgment. Ask McCormick whether his reaper has not had golden harvest ; Morse, whether the magnet has not attracted to him gold as well as iron ; Howe, whether the " tread " of the sewing-machine is not for him over pavement of coin.

A brief time before he closed, the shadows of the premature evening came over the hall. The light of day waned and faded·as I have seen it pass from the rich and varied tintings of cathedral windows. The great crowd, in shade, but not indistinct, heeded no departure of the day. To them and before them, the intellectual light had not set. Soon far up, nigh to the roof of the·hall, sprung into brilliancy one jet after another, till the vast building seemed to have put on a coronal of light. The statue of Beethoven received the lustre on its bronze drapery ; the upturned faces of the audience brightened, and a soft veil of light was over orator and hearer. The picture seemed suddenly painted, as accompaniment to the beauty of the words that were in utterance.

With the close of Mr. Everett's discourse, the great crowd rushed, delighted and instructed, to the pitiless north-easter, which roared and moaned in these streets, as though we were in the Fitful Head where Norna dwelt.

We are but as yesterday from the sight of the

national honors so gracefully accorded to **Mr. Everett** at his death. The more carefully cultured laurel of the historian will, in due time, be placed over his grave. In the memory of the hundreds of thousands, his voice will be their ideal of the beautiful in oratory; and in whatever department of human action he moved, a just estimate of him will concede, that he achieved success as useful as it was great.

Mr. Sheridan said that his own master passion was vanity,—that he could conquer all others. In the far-off look, but attentive, however distant, that I have had of the very great men of this country, I should say that it was just the reverse of this with them. They do not seem to have fully estimated the grandeur of their own position, and were annoyed or disturbed at the lesser causes which wound around them, without feeling (as the People felt and as History will make record) how vastly above all this their station in the truth of fame was. Even the majestic George Washington, who mingled very carefully with his fellow-men, was indignant at the articles about himself in the opposition newspapers; while Mr. Clay and Mr. Webster, with all their greatness, never saw, as the world around them saw clearly, and as is even now blazing in the light of history, how much greater honor the heart-given support of friends, than all the majorities the Electoral College ever heard figured; and Mr. Everett, so accomplished and cultured in the experiences of the world, was greatly provoked at the injustice of a portion of the press toward him, — annoyed at articles which nobody ever remembered. In a letter to me, he says: " What does a little surprise and a good deal grieve me is, that conservative and friendly journals, with a very few exceptions, look calmly on and see this unexampled warfare waged upon me, in violation of all the established rules of journalism. Pardon me this burst of human feeling. You have observed me long enough to know that I am tolerably impassive ; but the glacier at length melts."

17

CHAPTER VII.

F those who, at this day, hear the friends of Daniel Webster speak of him in terms of admiration, so warm and so earnest as to seem exaggerated, imagine that it is but in the distance of the years that such things are said; that it is only in the mist of time, which conceals defect and brightens virtue, that he is seen as a colossal man; they do the judgment and the accuracy of those friends injustice. While Mr. Webster lived,— as he moved majestically among men, in his progress to and from Washington, in his seat in the Senate, in his chair at the State office, at Marshfield, in Beacon Street, at the Astor House,— everywhere Mr. Webster was surrounded by a company of attached, devoted, absorbed men, who *knew* that they were the friends, chosen and cherished, of a man who, in intellectual strength, had not his equal in all the wide, wide New World; and in their friendship, they were. sacrificing, persevering, unchanging. They believed that the Presidency was due to him, and for it they waged a contest which ended only as his life ended. I saw these devoted friends at the Convention of 1852, at Baltimore. They labored with a zeal and a courage that was proudest of all tributes to the grandeur of the man who could deserve or win such service. What a scene that was when Choate was selected to make the champion speech, which should tell the nation of the public service of the man around whom they clustered like the men of Moidart around Charlie! That wildly picturesque face, its brilliant eye,— the face that would have been seen and noticed in a crowd of ten thousand,— how boldly that voice called the tumultuous Convention to the order of the fixed attention that eloquence extorts even from those who shut their hearts to the truth!

I ought to remember well, and I do so, when I first saw Daniel Webster; for his, certainly, is one of the greatest of the historic names of the annals of this country. June 17, 1843, was selected as the time when the top-stone was to be placed on the Monument at Bunker Hill. It was, as it might be said, the sunset hour of revolutionary association. It was expected to be the last, the final, the farewell gathering of those who had been the living and moving, the struggling and the suffering actors in that day, which, as we now see it, opened a new era in the movements of mankind, and initiated a new epoch.

Among those whom I found travelling toward Boston, I found, coming into the cars at Cayuga Bridge, Josiah Cleveland, who had acted as ensign in the field of the battle day, and who, at the siege and capitulation of Yorktown, had been captain. He was a man of imposing presence, firm and commanding way, with costume in fitting taste for an aged man. He was then ninety years of age. The home of his old age was on the banks of the Susquehanna, at Owego, near the sweet cottage, Glen Mary, made famous by Mr. Willis' interesting delineation of its incidents as his residence. Mr. Cleveland came into the cars, and when asked, by some one in the train, where he was going,—" To Bunker Hill," said he, promptly, as recognizing only the geography of the Revolution. His was a long journey for one so old, yet he bore it, continued as it was all night, and he reached Boston safely,— reached it, never to return from it. The reaction, after all the fatigue, ended his life. He was buried at Mount Auburn, and the liberality of some of the liberal men of Boston gave him appropriate monument, which is to-day one of the very many interesting sepulchral records of that fairest of all the grave-homes of the land.

The day before the festival, the 16th, was a gloomy one. The hotels, and indeed all Boston, were crowded, and it rained savagely, just as it can rain on the seacoast, where the east wind seems the cup-bearer to the earth, and fond of its duty of libation. " Shall to-morrow be as this day ? " was the question which citizen and stranger asked ; and we studied the sky with an earnestness which is the characteristic of that department of meteorology whose problem is but to solve the time of the vapor.

We were somewhat enlivened by the arrival of President Tyler, who, when he came, certainly did not find a dry eye in the assemblage that surrounded his carriage. He was surrounded by his cabinet, of whom the most resistless intellect was our own John C. Spencer. Legré, of South Carolina, the brilliant and eloquent scholar and civilian, came also, and never returned, — as he found, in that time of festivity, the appointed time for his mortality.

There were, also, arrivals of private gentlemen, who had celebrity of association. Among these was the venerable Nicholas Van Rensselaer, of Greenbush, opposite Albany, the gentleman who was, in 1777, selected by General Schuyler to act as the aide-de-camp in escort of General Burgoyne from Saratoga to the superb hospitality of the Schuyler mansion at Albany..

The 17th came, and somewhere I heard a band playing the barque carol, "Behold how brightly breaks the morning!" and it was so true, that we could have embraced that band from bassoon to triangle. Boston was instantly radiant. The Common gleamed green glories in its freshly-bathed verdure, and everywhere flags floated and bayonets glittered, and the people of the city seemed relieved; having, probably, as is the case with most of us in our home-gala days, taken upon themselves the conduct of the weather as an individual responsibility. The atmosphere had been pleasantly cooled by the rain, and there were just clouds enough, in the beautiful blue above us, to curtain off the summer sun. It was a day for a great *fête,* and the people accepted the delightful gift.

In the morning, the President held levee at the Tremont. Boston had prepared for the Chief Magistrate of the United States a luxurious suite of rooms. We read, as from the Court Circular, of the damask and marbles and chandeliers and vases and claret and gold and green of the ornaments and decorations. I do not mean to condemn this. At that time it was less in the line of life, public or private, to be as ornate, but our plain and simple theory is but a theory. The taste for display, for magnificence, *is* in the people. It is so in wedding procession to the chancel, in funeral *cortége* to the tomb.

At the levee I saw Colonel Miller, whose name is famous in the history of the war of 1812, because, when General Jacob Brown asked him if he would take a certain battery, his modest answer (followed by his successful storming of it) was, " I'll try, sir," — words which became a motto of soldierly daring.

There was something of English arrangements for the seeing of the procession. Eligible places were offered to rent. I noticed that a very convenient gallery of this kind was ingeniously placed on a part of the " Old South," which, if it was intended to accommodate the minister and elders of that time-honored sanctuary, showed an anxiety for the care of the hierarchy well becoming the City of the Pilgrims.

There was the utmost order in the crowd which awaited the procession's coming. It was like the order in the streets of Montreal as the Prince of Wales moved through, and like the good regulation of the streets of Albany as the funeral pageant of the murdered President was borne along. Every window of every house along the line of the route was thronged, from the paper pasteboard to the plate glass. I was amused at seeing the perplexed toll-gatherer of Warren Bridge endeavoring to collect his lawful dues from each pedestrian, while the vast crowd, in so many ways, went all around him.   The Revenue Cutter, Captain Sturgis, beautifully decorated with flags, was moored at the precise spot, where, on the day of the battle, the British vessel, the Glasgow, lay, and from whence it cannonaded the Heights.   Among other banners, this vessel bore the famous old pine-tree banner of ancient Massachusetts.

Just at the side of the monument, which, in excellent taste, had no other decoration than four flags pointing to each compass direction, was arranged an immense amphitheatre of seats, which were already thronged with the daughters of the land, who had come at an early hour, and who, whatever might be their faint chance of seeing, had the luxury of being seen; and this is a chapter in the great book of the compensations of life, which deserves to be looked at very carefully and written about ingeniously.

Some of the sovereign people did not relish the military discipline which kept the space open and clear till the arrival of the President.   I was amused at the quaint remark of an old gentleman, who had been made to walk out of the forbidden ground in gentle quick time, that there were " as many slaves here as there were on the day of the battle."

The scene at the Monument was of the great pictures that history paints : the blue sky above,—

the mighty Monument seeking the upper air, its four streamers pointing to every quarter of this free land, the colors of star and stripe exquisitely in contrast with the azure of the heavens, — at the base of the Monument all the different hues of the varied dresses of the thousands of ladies, — a garden of living flowers.

Mr. Webster felt the impulse of the hour ; and its incidents would have stirred the living heart of any man ; certainly of him who was selected from amidst all the nation to speak the words that should enshrine that hour. The crowd before him was vast. It was a great gathering from lands remote and near ; for, to this hour, the attention of the whole people had been awakened. The President of the United States and his cabinet were at his side. It was the homage of the power of place to the power of mind. And he was surrounded also by those whom only this scene could have delayed in their movement to the grave. The vicinage of the opening battle-fields of the Revolution were represented by numbers whose feeble life energies culminated in the effort to reach this day and place. There were one hundred and eleven veritable revolutionary soldiers present. Of these, the youngest man was seventy-four. (*He* must have been a *very* young soldier, if he took part in the Revolution.) Four of them, — the Harringtons,

Bigelow, and Johnson, — had been in the opening skirmishes of Concord and Lexington, — those morning guns of a long roll of war, which has had faint and few intervals of silence from that hour.

I am a little incredulous about revolutionary certificates, — but one of these men, Levi Harrington, seems to have been of the two who signed a brief note mentioning April 25, 1775, the Lexington affair.

There was a preliminary prayer, made by a gentleman who had written a history of the battle. When the corner-stone, in 1824, was laid, the opening prayer was made by the Rev. Mr. Thaxter, who, fifty years previous, as chaplain of Prescott's regiment, had made the prayer just before the fight. In 1824, he was the only survivor of the regiment; the hearers of his former prayer were all in the grave; he and the Being whom he addressed were alone.

There was great kindness shown to visitors on this occasion, and I found, through the kindness of Josiah Quincy, Jr., a place on the platform, where I could write, and from whence I could see Mr. Webster very distinctly. His sentences were so well made, having such completeness of arrangement, that he was an easy man to report; but my attention was drawn from the words to the orator. He had the sagacity,— for, in Mr. Webster there always seemed to be plan and purpose, and hence I could not use the word *tact*, as I should in the case of Mr. Clay,— he had the sagacity to avail himself of all the positions of the day, of what it presented to oratory; so he made glowing welcome to the old soldiers; he was grand about the battle, about our nationality; he declared that, in the event of the dissolution of the Union, he would avert his eyes from it forever. He aroused, to all the grandeur of a demonstration, the crowd, by his bright words concerning Washington. At this word of love and honor concerning the grand old Virginian, the tumultuous plaudits of the crowd could not be restrained, and somebody shouted out, " Three cheers, three cheers all over the world! " A proposition which the then densely-crowded area of Bunker Hill agreed to, and fulfilled to the strength of their voices; and the sound of a mighty multitude has always in it the majestic.

So soon as the oration was concluded, the President of the United States rose, and, as I thought at the time of observing it, very gracefully congratulated Mr. Webster; and his example was followed by his cabinet; and throughout the concourse there was a stir and a sensation, as if they had been in themselves somewhat of history that day.

There was a great banquet, in the evening, at Faneuil Hall; and without departing from the limitations of this work, it is curious record to make, that, on that occasion, the toast given by President Tyler was, " The Union,—union of purpose, union of feeling,—the Union established by our fathers." The toast given almost at the initiative of the feast, was, " South Carolina and Massachusetts,— shoulder to shoulder they went through the Revolution, laying up for each other great treasures of glory ; the sons never will divide the great inheritance." And Mr. Upshur, of Virginia, the then Secretary of the Treasury, gave, as his sentiment, " Massachusetts,— foremost in the conflict by which our liberties were won, and foremost to show us what our liberties are when won."

A day so magnificent, its celebration became a renewed era in the history of Boston. The old soldiers went home to die ; the Monument was completed record, and the last chapter of Revolutionary companionship was finished.

Mr. Webster was a man who, to such a prepared and anticipated event, would bring all the intellectual power that the hour required. He was best in these, because he prepared with full sense of the value of that which was before him as his duty, and he thought of the after-study of his words ; and hence it was his design that they should be worthy of that study. Mr. Clay thought of the effect ; and the one saw mankind as his students,— the other, as his soldiers. Mr. Webster had greater ideas of the dignity of reason. Mr. Clay desired to mould the men before him to his sway, and in their impulses his own kindled and grew larger and greater. I have heard Mr. Webster when I did not especially care to hear longer at that time. I never heard Mr. Clay but that all else, hunger or occupation, was forgotten in the wish to hear more from *him*.

I saw Mr. Webster enter the superbly decorated dining-room of the Astor House, when a banquet was given by the St. Nicholas Society to the officers, of a Netherlands man-of-war, and, heralded by the graceful and winning voice of Ogden Hoffman, itself a perpetual pleasure, he rose to the hour in wise and worthy word of welcome to the Hollander ; and so, that evening, the mariners of the land that has to fight the sea itself, saw and heard the best representative of New England, and the brightest and most distinguished of those whose ancestors had thought it a pleasant filial tribute to give the land to which Hendrick Hudson had piloted them, the name of New Netherlands.

For such a scene as this, Ogden Hoffman was most felicitous of chairmen. As the Scotch ballad says,—

· " His very voice had music in it,"

and he knew what word was most in unison with the sparkle of the hour. " Often, often," said he, " have we had in our festivals brilliants, jewelry of intellect, but never, till this hour, could I present to you, as I do now, the Koh-i-noor, the Mountain of Light!" And then rose Webster, and, with that grandly grave superiority which so well became *him*, centred at once the attention of all. I doubt not our guests, in their quiet houses by the dykes, often recall that evening; and, as they remember its hospitalities, breathe kindly wish for the welfare of those who would not forget that something in them yet toned to the memories or the traditions of the land that loves and fears the ocean.

That was a famous evening when Mr. Webster presided over the assembled literati, who gathered to do honor to the memory of America's greatest author, James Fennimore Cooper. I think it was very honorable to Mr. Webster that he was thus called to preside, for the guild of letters had many high and honorable names in their own right, there assembled. Dressed in that buff and blue, which belonged to him, as thoroughly as one of these colors was the badge of those fast friends of Mr. Fox, who were toasted by Mrs. Crewe, he was soon interested in the scene, as all the audience were in him; and as Mr. Irving, just as quick as

possible, made brief announcement of the purposes
of the evening, the Statesman called forth the
men whose names were the head and front and
heart of the literature of America.

I saw him at the time,— a worn, wasted old
man,— coming slowly down the staircase of the
Astor House. It was the other side to the grand
Statesman, and the equipage of the evening, rising,
by the strength of his broad and philosophical intellect, above all the rank that letters confer. Perhaps it was not in all the proprieties of the event,
that any other but a great author should have
been the leading mind in the funeral honor of the
author who had established for his country so high
a place in the world's literature; yet it was to be
seen in another light, and in that view where could
the greatest Statesman of the Union be most appropriately prominent, but at this tribute to the
greatest of the literary men of the Republic.

I left Mr. Clay's side (and I speak this of myself only because I believe that in it I represented
the mass who stood around me) willing to do anything, be anything, he wished me to do, or that
would win triumph for him. I left Mr. Webster
strong, and convinced that he had the right and
deserved the victory; but there might be doubt
about the full duty of self-sacrifice to promote that
end.

I regret that I never saw Mr. Calhoun, because he was, in the universal acceptation of his day, a man who deserved the first place among statesmen. Those who knew him tell me of the intense devotion to him personally which characterized his followers, and that, when he died, the leading men who had made him their master, indicated all the personal sorrow that, of old, the clans had in the hour of the passing away of a chieftain.

To no man is there such universal testimony of wonderful power given as has reached me on all sides concerning the oratory of Sargeant S. Prentiss. It is fame of the highest order to be avouched, as he has been, in the grandeur of eloquence, of that might of the intellect which made the multitude, educated or unlearned, confess their willing thraldom. Mr. Everett described to me interestingly the great effect which Prentiss produced on himself when he first heard him at Faneuil Hall; and, said Mr. Everett, I heard him at the close of a fatigued dinner, when others who had preceded him had taken more than their share of the time, and I turned to Mr. Webster, who sat next me, to express my delight, and Mr. Webster declared that *Prentiss was always thus.* Equal praise proceeded to him from Charles King, whose life has given him the best opportunity to hear the best men. When Prentiss was dis-

covered as a passenger on board of one of the
Mississippi steamboats, at a side-river town, the
crowd insisted on his speaking. He addressed
them ; and the crowd were in the spell of the
magician as the engineer of the boat appeared and
declared that he had held the rush of the steam
back as long as was possible to prevent interruption by the noise, and that it *must* now escape, or
the boiler burst. All the answer he got from
the charmed crowd was, " Let it burst."

Of the Bar, I saw most of those who gave
dignity to the profession, whose theory is, — the
most skilful and accurate analysis of proof, in evidence and fact, to develop the truth, — a theory,
which, like many texts in sermons, is preached
from. I was most impressed with William H.
Maynard, who died at the very initiation of the
career of a very great man. He was counsel in a
cause when I had an interest to see him unsuccessful ; but, in face of all my wishes, my justice
could not deny him the plaudit of greatness. He
seemed to be a master, adroit and learned, and of
that class of men who make reason of assertion, —
who so frame their words as that they are invinci-
ble in demonstration as they move on.

Nicholas Hill was a name of eminence beyond
its lustre in the circles of legal lore that form at
the Capitol, in the place where the highest judici-
18

ary sits in deliberation. In the study of every
counsellor in New York, and in many beyond the
confines of the great State, — indeed, of every one
conversant with the best of his great profession, —
the name of this gentleman was uttered with respect, indeed, with admiration, and the tidings
of his death — his clock of time ceasing its movement while yet the noon of intellect was at its
height — came like the sudden alarm of the night.
He died in the advance of his learning, and in the
onward step. The brain that admitted the fatal
heat of the fever was already warm with the glow
of study, and death came by the door which himself
had opened widest; and in the augmenting of the
treasures of his learning, he died amidst its accu-
mulations.

It was to me always a scene of interest to witness
the fixed attention with which the Court of Appeals listened to him. I so often see those wearied
and much-enduring eight forced to pay the homage
of the outward ear to counsel whose arguments
are but assertions, and points dulness, that to see
this exchanged for an impressed, interested deference is a relief. It is as if some indulgence had
been granted to the tasked laborer.

That court knew that Mr. Hill was a lawyer, in
the high sense of that word; that the flame *he* lit
before them was of beaten oil; that the argument

he formed for their consideration deserved it, and
that they might well tread that path of authorities,
to the doctrines and conclusions of which he cited
them.   They heard, as, of old, Spencer heard
Henry, as Van Ness heard Wells, as, in date more
remote, Jay heard Hamilton.   Rising above and
going beyond the hasty and half-considered conduct of a cause, rather than its preparation, Mr.
Hill revived the day of the sound student of the
law, who had, with that philosophy which is the
clear glass that learning in all departments of its
action uses, investigated, analyzed, *formed* the law,
and was able to enunciate all its truths.

Of pale, wan look, of feeble, shattered frame,
the paralyzed arm giving gesture of imperfect
movement, though of correct expression, he rose
before the court like one who knew the dignity of
the lawyer's art, and who knew, as observing men
must know, that the master of the law is the master of our nature.

What an array of counsel was gathered in the
great North American Trust Company case!
What side of many-sided legal propositions was
there but that light came on it thence ?   It was a
great gathering of the worthiest of those who
grace the roll of the civilians of New York.

Mr. Hill confined his practice to the highest
court, and wisely ; for study, such as he gave, was

remunerated only by a settlement of the question in review. He felt the majesty of the law. One of the last words I heard him utter was his remark to me, as we talked of some decision where the court had been compelled to exercise its most disagreeable power, that of declaring the interpretation of some patronage-making law of a partisan legislature. He expressed his belief that the decision of the court would find acquiescence. " We are a loyal people," said he. I did not · think he was so soon thereafter to illustrate the universal loyalty of our race, — the homage to the grave.

The life of William Curtis Noyes was closed in the zenith of his capacity to make it a most useful one. To have acted with him in the delineation of Mr. Storrs' career, would have been agreeable labor; for its association with himself would have made the hours to be remembered most kindly. I liked the way in which Mr. Noyes dignified his own profession. He believed in its chivalry, in tracing back its wisdom in the long roll of grand jurists, and he thought their words the heritage of our own time. He was lofty in his ambition concerning the law, and used the fine intellect he possessed to make the place of the first counsel in the metropolis — if such honor he should ever attain — something of a dignity, which, though robeless and unermined, should be a name for the respect of all men.

Some of the most famous of the world-wide travellers I have seen. It would, probably, be a more valuable recollection, if I could state which of the two pioneers of the trans-Mississippi West, Lewis or Clarke, a venerable man, with whom the chances of packet-boat journeying brought me. He was pointed out at the time as worthy of a distinct gaze.

I met, at Cincinnati, a gentleman who recollected well, that when he was of the number of those who formed an unsuccessful expedition to accomplish the passage of the Yellow Stone river, Daniel Boone came down to the wharf,— a gentle, dignified, impressive old man,— to see the steamboat bound on an expedition so far beyond the utmost limit to which his step, so bold in all adventure that could prepare the way for civilization, had reached.

John L. Stephens, who wrote that delightful book of travel in the Holy Land, was a genial and very agreeable gentleman, much more in his vocation as a traveller and an author, than in the dusty ways of statesmanship, where, as a member of the Constitutional Convention of 1846, I saw much of him. He had the kindly way of a man who has seen more than one chapter of human life, and I think had less of that cynicism, that universal doubt of everybody, which appertains to great travellers, who, in the general wrong. or insufficiency, forget that they have passed through life rather than dwelt in it.

But the name among travellers which is best , known, by its deeply shadowed fate, is that of Sir John Franklin. While he was on his way overland to the North, and then, I believe, in the duty, which the whole civilized world has assumed respecting himself, of a search after somebody who overstayed his time, and who, it was feared, was in great want of food or warmth somewhere in the vast North,— I saw this distinguished adventurer at the rooms of the Albany Library.

I believe the Albany Library rose out of a collection of books made by the officers of Fort Orange and Fort Frederick, in the day when those fortresses were the temporary home of the educated English army officer, whose range of feasting and flirtation was not so·great as to preclude the coming over him of *ennui*. Whether I am right in this idea of its origin or not, at the hour when the great Northman visited it, it was situated in the upper story of a building since removed by the city, to give greater width to the river-end of State Street, or else in the space now included by the Exchange. It was before the ambition of Albany required a

broader State Street; and the ascent to this deposit
of literature was by a narrow and steep staircase,
in ascending which the juveniles had the great advantage, and of which, in a progress for the last
" Waverley," that treasure always, we were not
slow to avail ourselves.   The librarian had the
very name for profundity,— an unpronounceable
German one.   He was clever, that is, obliging,
although not insensible to the annoyance of successive journeys to all the shelves, to suit the tastes
of those visitors who, not finding " in " Ivanhoe or
Rob Roy, and not having come with their literary
appetite prepared for any other food, mumbled very
miscellaneously.   *We* knew just where the books
were kept; we were *habitués*, and were indulged,
sometimes, I believe, to such luxury as to be
allowed the privilege of leaping over the counter,
and, by personal search, gratifying a taste that
watched the arrival of every new book, " and
there were giants in those days."

It was while we were thus in predatory attendance on the librarian, that we saw enter the room,
attended by a gentleman who then held distinguished representative place in the National Government, a grave, rather sad-looking gentleman,
practical, compact, and dignified, who was made
known to the custodian of the books, as Captain
John Franklin.

Like sensible boys, we turned from the written history to the living one ; for the reputation of Captain Franklin, as an Arctic traveller, was recognized, and Parry's voyages had made all reading people enthusiasts about whatever should find way into the crystal caverns of the Far North. He had been led to the library to consult an ancient black-covered volume, which was remembered by us as an old settler on the shelves,— one of those books which, like the works of the philosophers of Athens, everybody admires at a distance. Its subject was the form of the earth, and it had maps or charts which professed delineation of the near and remote portions of the globe. Captain Franklin seemed to understand, at a glance, that it presented no fact, in its lines and figures, which could aid him, for he made a very brief inspection of the volume. Fortunately for us, he was at the room long enough for us to obtain a careful look at him ; and it must have been an earnest impression, for, from that hour, my recollection of him has always been that of a man rather grave to sadness. I am sure I do not know why this should have been so then, for no seer stood at his side to tell him that, amidst starving followers and death-cold men, the then far-off summer days of 1847 should bring him to his grave ; while, living or dead, the whole Christian world was giving

wealth, and even life itself, to his rescue ; and that
Heaven was to smile over the most rare Christian
union of England and the United States and
France in a work of love of mán for his fellow-
man. I should have gazed on him even more
earnestly had I thought that in him such high
humanity was to concentrate. Does any citizen
of Albany know " what has become " of the book
which he at that time consulted ?

Alexander Vattemare was a traveller of rare
experiences,— a peculiar and rather an eccentric
man, but very energetic and very persevering, and
the cause of pleasant and profitable embassages of
literature from one to the other of nations. President, Emperor, Pope, King, and Czar were all his
agents in furnishing to the libraries of each other
the best books,— that is, the costly national volumes, — which their liberality prepared. He
claimed to be the real author of the great Interna-
tional Exhibitions, and told me that it was a chapter in the world's injustice, that Prince Albert
should have received so much commendation for
this. He was an interesting talker. In the early
period of his life, — as M. Alexander, — he had ac-
quired great celebrity as a ventriloquist, and received the homage of an address, in verse, from
Sir Walter Scott; but even this, of which any
man might have been proud, did not seem to recon-

cile him to any association with these memories.
In his Album Cosmopolitique, there was abundant
evidence that he had been a very successful and
popular man.   I recollect there was a superb portraiture of his daughter, whom he seemed to guard
carefully from association with his ventriloquial
career.

On one occasion he accompanied me to examine, at my request, a superb engraving of the
celebrities of the Court of Napoleon.   He looked
at them, but soon desisted, declaring that they painfully revived old memories.   In a man of less real
experience in the saloons of monarchs, this might
have been a little out of taste, or absurd, but it
was excusable in him.   Returning up Lydius
Street, Albany, that evening, in its shadows we
saw the Roman Catholic cathedral, then in erec-
tion.   I shall never forget the truly Gallic expression he used, in speaking of the size of the
building.   He stopped, looked at it, seemed impressed with its dimensions.   " That is a very
large church," said he, and made a short pause;
" *but it could dance in some of ours in Paris.*"

He told me he had seen twenty-eight kings; and
after seeing thus about all there is on earth to see,
he died, best remembered as having been the
means of giving wider scope to the governmental
literature of the nations of the earth,— a healthy
and useful and honorable fame.

I have heard that strange and useless visionary, Robert Owen, as he lectured on his problems of a better time coming for all men, — himself forgetting, that in the wisdom which he neglected was the only guide to the happiness he proposed. There was nothing attractive about him as a lecturer ; and but for his reputation, one would not have cared to listen. He was permitted to use the Assembly chamber for his discourse, and he lived on in a hope of seeing a world coming to his theory.

Why did he go thus about among nations that he must have seen rode under or over his theories every day ? Are not many theoretical-talking reformers, in their resultless efforts, only dispelling that within them which Miss Martineau calls "inborn *ennui.*"

Is not the calm life of quiet, which may not be heard beyond the walls of its earthly home, often of greater usefulness? There may be power, resistless power, in that which Lady Churchill's epitaph, at Lincoln, characterizes as a " gentle wafting to immortal life." Truth and steadfastness, in the smallest circle of friends, has a value that is beyond great-reaching theories. I would rather see a child's look toward its mother than to hear lukewarm philosophy " crying to the moon and stars for impossible sympathy."

There were some, most favored, individuals who brought back to us their recollections of Walter

Scott, that greatest of writers since the Bard of
Avon (which latter exception is made as black
mail to the world's opinion, and not because I
think so). I heard Mr. Irving's narrative of his
unequalled days passed in the magician's own
home-spell; and Mr. George Ticknor's testimony
to the fidelity of the original portrait of Sir Walter,
which is over his hearth, and of which Mrs. Lockhart said to Mr. Ticknor, that she could not for-
givê him for bearing away to America the best
portrait of her father. Mr. Cobden told me, that
when he visited Edinburgh, he made it his very
grateful duty to find the great author; and in
searching for him, in his place at the Court, he
discovered, after being directed to the sheriff, a '
heavy and not bright-looking gentleman at the
desk, absorbed in clerical duties, and apparently
not interested in what the Court was doing, till a
sudden illumination of his face, at a wise or witty
thing that was said by counsellor or judge, revealed the genius.

But a queer testimony to the liberal hospitality
of Abbotsford was related to me by a man whom I
found in one of our western villages, and who
claimed often to have seen Sir Walter. I, at first,
doubted, thinking that such recollection might be
the great card of all Scotchmen, and that it was
prudent to cross-examine a little before listening to

the relation. He claimed to be a son of the butcher at Melrose, and the suggestion gave a very practical and work-day coloring to the moon-lit Abbey. " Yes," said he, " I often saw him. They ate a power of meat at Abbotsford, — often a whole sheep and sometimes a lamb."

I was forced to believe in the story of another Scotchman, a stone-mason, who claimed to have assisted in the building of Abbotsford, by his saying, that " it was a house of a great many corners," for this delineation of its wayward architecture was too faithful to be doubted.

These are all meagre incidents of any companionship with those who knew Scott, by look or conversation, personally ; but even these I cherished. It was a positive delight to look at that portrait in Mr. Ticknor's library, for it reflected the very man ; and I think the curiosity of all men, that have a real love for literature, is intense yet to know all about him. Lockhart's biography, admirable indeed, is yet a cold-blooded affair, and does not frame the generous and glad man in such coloring as his kind nature gave him title to.

What a succession of triumphs the Waverleys ! What books ever were there which so imbued the mind of all men ! The acquaintance with them was the shibboleth of society, and he who could not appreciate or accept an apt quotation from them, as they came to the delighted public, was declared a dull fellow. They were intensely sought; and a gentleman who was an *habitué* of the bookstore of John Wiley, who, at New York, republished them, declared to me that when, by the cleverness of Mr. Wiley, he was permitted to read them at the counter, it was with difficulty he could retain a volume long enough to compass the story, such was the eagerness of the purchasers. I recollect there was a ludicrous spasm of fashion about the pronunciation of the title, Ivanhoe, — all very plain to us, — but then public opinion divided into parties of accent on the first, second, or third syllable; while the extreme in fashion declared for a peculiar twisting and Gallicism of each division of the word, so that it should sound something like E-vanwe. That work obliterated the work of Cervantes, and its ideas are yet fibres of the world's language.

Although, as I now read the two series of books, I cannot see how any one could doubt that he who wrote the poems wrote the romances; yet, in the day of the " Great Unknown " fiction, the doubt was a very serious one, — so much so, that when a placard of advertisement of " Scott's New Novel," was in some bookseller's window in State Street, in Albany, it was thought an unauthorized declaration.

One of the best evidences of the power Scott held over the public thought, and the deep feeling toward him, is in the tablet raised to his memory in the wall of the City Hall in Albany,— a place as devoid of all romance as the dustiest of the didactic could desire ; but there it is, and it does honor to the citizens of Albany. Where else in the country is there a remembrance, in civic edifice, of an author, and he a far-off one, and one who wrote of peers and princes, of rank and chivalry, of themes utterly removed from our everyday life ? But the spell was on the people. Scott had covered the mind of the country with a gold that was better than leaf or tinsel.

There was a public meeting, held at the Mansion House, to testify the public grief at his death. Harmanus Bleecker presided, and declared his admiration of his virtue as of his intellect ; but afterwards said to me that, if he had known then that Sir Walter had absolutely denied the authorship of the romances, he doubted if he should have been authorized to speak so strongly of his integrity. Mr. Bleecker was a high-thoughted man, who could not understand any compromise with the truth. I think the justice of the case was, that Sir Walter had no right to deny, as he did, but nobody had any right to ask him the question.

The last page of these memories comes, — not that their theme is exhausted, but that it may not be 'wise to take this place of remembrance, — and it is well to test it carefully. How many men have I known die, — how many men live on, in avoidance or neglect of the duty they owe their fellowmen, — who possessed and retain the most delightful recollections of the great men and great events which their wandering over the world, or their public service, have made them to know. I am sure I have labored with some of them, that they should do, as they could so charmingly, what I, from materials gathered in a limited circle, have endeavored to do in this volume. Silas Wright once said, if he ever should again begin the world, he would give more attention to writing than he had done, as more influential than speaking.

Were that gift of life renewed to me, certainly one use of the treasure that I would make, would be to make record of what I saw and heard; and thus really see and hear that wonderful drama — which is always acting before us — our own life I should better learn that, with all the shadows of its errors, even a common life is a theme worthy of an angel's study.

www.ingramcontent.com/pod-product-compliance
Lightning Source LLC
Chambersburg PA
CBHW021045030726
47496CB00006B/1693